ANYTHING
Can Happen
in High School

(and it usually does)

ANYTHING
Can Happen
in High School
(and it usually does)

William D. McCants

BROWNDEER PRESS

HARCOURT BRACE & COMPANY

San Diego   New York   London

Library of Congress Cataloging-in-Publication Data
McCants, William D., 1961–
Anything can happen in high school: (and it
usually does)/by William D. McCants.—1st ed.
p. cm.
"Browndeer Press."
Summary: Staggered by the loss of his girlfriend,
Janet, fifteen-year-old T.J. starts a service club,
the Radical Wave, to attract school outsiders,
provide community involvement, and win Janet back.
ISBN 0-15-276604-9.—ISBN 0-15-276605-7 (pbk.)
[1. High schools—Fiction. 2. Schools—Fiction.
3. Clubs—Fiction. 4. Humorous stories.] I. Title.
PZ7.M47836An 1993
[Fic]—dc20   92-32982

Design by Camilla Filancia
Printed in Hong Kong
First edition   A B C D E

To Annie

ANYTHING
Can Happen
in High School

(and it usually does)

One "She dumped me!" I shouted in disbelief as I hung up the phone. I'd given Janet Brooks the best three months of my life, and she'd dumped me. This was a disaster! I'd be starting the new school year with a broken heart, which was like starting up Mount Everest in cement shoes.

"Did you hear me?" I asked my best friend, Alex, as he worked on his second bowl of Sugar-Frosted Flakes.

He nodded solemnly, trying to look sympathetic as a thin stream of milk dribbled down his chin.

"Ungrateful female slime," he said after he'd swallowed.

I picked up a computer-game cartridge and threw it at him. It knocked his Dodger cap off. "Don't talk that way about Janet," I said illogically.

"Hey," he said, "this is *my* trailer."

It was, for all practical purposes, his trailer. He technically shared the place with his mother, but between her job at the phone company and her habit of staying over at her

1

boyfriend's house for days at a time, Alex pretty much had it all to himself. (And he seemed to like it that way.)

I apologized to my host.

I almost wanted to cry as I thought about how Janet'd probably never come over to this trailer again. She'd never have another chance to make fun of the junk furnishings Alex and I had made from stuff we'd collected on the beach—like the orange plastic lobster float that became a lamp, or the toilet seat that'd been lovingly carved out of driftwood.

Alex was standing beside me now, his pale, freckled face regarding me with concern. "Are you okay, T.J.?" he asked. "You look like you're going to cry or something."

"No way," I assured him as I wiped my eyes on my shirtsleeve. "It's the smell in here that's getting to me. You need to buy some more of those industrial-strength air-fresheners."

"Let's go to my office and talk," he said sympathetically, "man to basket-case." I was slow in getting up because I was feeling a little green. Of course, if I'd *known* Janet was going to dump me this evening, I'd've had something more nutritious for dinner than two bowls of cold cereal, a stack of chocolate-chip cookies, and a couple of lemon-lime sodas.

We walked about three feet into Alex's living room and collapsed onto the zebra-striped couch. The couch was a real find. It'd been abandoned under a freeway overpass in Long Beach. There was a Persian rug fragment on the floor in front of the couch that probably had been trashed when Ali Baba was in high school. Across the frazzled sea of stained, faded carpet, an ancient TV set rested uncertainly on an "entertainment center" made from reinforced cardboard. The TV antennas were set at an angle of precisely fifty-two degrees, which allowed Alex to get clear reception on exactly one network station. (Of course, it was the one with the lamest shows.) This had not mattered so much when Alex had a VCR, but his mom had taken the vital video machine over to her boyfriend's house one fateful weekend and had somehow forgotten to bring it back.

"I'd better eat something healthy before we talk, Alex," I told him, clutching my gut. "I feel like I'm going to puke. Do you have some cheese or anything with protein in it?"

He nodded and went back into the kitchen

to rummage through his milk-white 1950s-vintage refrigerator. I heard him crank up the microwave. He returned in a few minutes with a plate of nacho-cheese-flavored tortilla chips smothered with melted cheese, salsa, and sour cream. "This'll put the fire back into your gut," he declared as he set the goods before me.

I thanked him and began to munch out. Maybe I could replace heartbreak with heartburn. Alex guzzled down a Coke, then let out a belch that tested the soundness of the trailer walls. "Let me lay it out for you, bud," he said. "Janet used you to win the election last spring, rewarded you with a summer romance, and then dumped you in time for the fall semester."

I worried over this theory for a few seconds, and then I shook my head. "That's *way* too cynical. I don't buy it."

He crumpled up his Coke can and threw it into the decapitated beer keg he used as a recycling bin. "So what's the story, then?"

"She said she thought things were getting way too intense with us, and she just couldn't deal with that kind of relationship right now. She also said I had a sarcastic streak about a mile wide, and that, while I was a great critic and everything, my negative attitude kept me from doing anything *constructive* to solve the problems I complained about."

Alex smiled crookedly. He was wearing round, blue-tinted glasses, and his hair was a wild, reddish brown firestorm. (He had the kind of soulful, rebel look that usually got him a date when he wanted one. But he hadn't yet committed to any long-term relationship. He was still looking for a girl who was "heavy, deep, and real.")

"But she's not being fair!" I continued. "I mean, she was getting *creamed* by Chuck MacQuarrie before I offered her my services as campaign manager. That slimeball was tearing down her posters faster than she could put them up. *And* he was spreading rumors that she was a mindless Barbie bimbo who was trying to use her wealth and blond-haired, blue-eyed good looks to coast into office. Full-on lies! If that crook had won the election and become sophomore class president, I think I would've transferred to a military school."

But as Alex knew, Chuck hadn't won—*we had*. At the election assembly debate, Janet had nailed Chuck for his nebulous, ridiculously impractical plans for class activities in the coming year. We turned the bimbo thing into a sexism issue, which put Chuck on the defensive, and Janet also made a speech championing more grass-roots student involvement in meeting community needs. She threw a Say No to Drugs rock/rap concert at lunch in the quad and even ran a campaign commercial on school TV. No one had ever done that before!

Alex was laughing at me. "And how'd she know you could put her over the top? Because the *imaginary* candidate you ran for freshman class president last fall almost won the damn election!"

I started laughing, too, as I remembered *that* great campaign. Back then Alex and I were just two dorky new freddies looking to raise some hell at Westport High. We succeeded in a big way but also made a busload of powerful enemies. *We* thought it was hilarious that an imaginary 200-pound freshman named "Big Wave Dave" could pull in almost thirty percent of the vote in a three-way race by promising to draw up a more liberal dress code and a new curriculum requiring, among other things, that teachers hold Friday classes at the beach. But the Student Leadership Council didn't think our campaign was funny at all, especially when the votes were tallied. The council practically begged the principal, Dr. Fremont, to suspend us, but he finally let us off with a warning to "show greater respect for the democratic process."

"Listen," I said, coming back to the present, "that's all ancient history. What does it have to do with *now*?"

"I'm just pointing out the obvious, O poor unfortunate one. You're a natural-born salesman, dude, sarcasm and all—and that's exactly what Janet needed when she was running for office." Alex paused to shove a handful of salsa-laden chips into his mouth. After munching for a moment, he continued, "You helped her become a high school superstar, and she loved you for it. But she didn't *love* you for it."

"Did she tell you that?" I asked, sitting bolt upright with anger.

He shook his head. "She doesn't talk to the likes of me. I'm too lowbrow for her, and so are you," he said calmly.

I stood up. "I've gotta go," I said.

"Whoa!" he said, holding up his hands, "Cool your jets, *hombre*. I'm on *your* side."

It dawned on me that Alex probably had no idea what I was going through. He was clueless, not insensitive. So I sat back down.

"Okay," he continued. "So, thanks in large part to your political skills, Janet gets elected at the end of last year and starts hanging out with the leadership crowd. She drags you along with her, but you don't really fit in. Her friends aren't your friends, and vice-versa. You have less and less in common. Then she goes to summer leadership camp. She's breaking bread and making beds with the elite of Westport High. It's the final nail in the coffin. And who knows? Maybe Associated Student Body President David Whitworth took more than a casual interest in Janet. Would you like some ice cream, by the way?"

David Whitworth? I'd met him at a party earlier in the summer. He was an obnoxious, silver-tongued senior who drove a red Beemer convertible and came from a filthy rich family that built tony shopping malls. Why was a magazine-model-perfect pervert like him going after a sweet, innocent sophomore like my Janet? And why hadn't she told me about him? She'd stabbed me in the back! I'd make her sorry!

"What kind of ice cream do you want, T.J.? By the look on your face, I'd guess you'll need about half a gallon," Alex said. There was already a spoon sticking out of his mouth.

As a rule, he kept at least five varieties of ice cream in his freezer. That left little room for meat and vegetables, but no sacrifice was too great where ice cream was concerned.

"Something chocolate!" I said urgently. (That future M.B.A. would be running his manicured nails through Janet's silky blond hair, smelling her floral perfumes, kissing her neck, walking her dogs. . . . It was just too horrible to think about.)

I was on my second bowl of Ben & Jerry's New York Super Fudge Chunk before I could speak coherently again. "How could this happen?" I asked hopelessly. "What'll I do?"

"Hey, you're a reasonably good-looking, funny kind of guy," Alex said. "Find a girl who thinks so. But stay away from Ocean Avenue princesses. Janet is no longer the geeky wallflower she was when you two first became friends. She's what's called a 'major babe' now, and you've been left in her proverbial dust. She's popular, you're not—but so what? Who needs to be popular," he asked, gesturing at his surroundings, "when you have a best friend with a trailer?"

I looked at him with disgust. "Your sympathy overwhelms me, Alex. I've been dumped and betrayed by the love of my life, and you can do nothing but insult me. You're *slime*. What kind of cookies do you have?"

"Oreos," he said.

We crumbled them and then sprinkled them over our ice cream like it was some kind of holy ritual.

"I'm going to get her back," I declared after a while. I reached into the kitchen and pulled a chair away from the fractured faux marble Formica table so that I'd have something to rest my legs on. (Alex and I were still waiting for someone to leave a coffee table under a freeway overpass in Long Beach.)

He shook his head with disgust and said, "There you go again. Look, she's not worth it. She dumped you for David Whitworth, a guy whose hair has never needed combing, an android who stepped on the corporate ladder in the first grade. We're growing up, T.J. We're dividing into our appropriate social classes. Janet's the service club, leadership council type. We join the language clubs and the science fiction societies because they're not so particular about who our parents know and what color their credit cards are."

But when Alex saw the expression on my face he said, "But hey, what do I know? Anything's possible."

He wasn't my best friend for nothing.

"Wait a minute," I said, getting mad again. "How long have you known about David Whitworth?"

He shook his head. "You hear all kinds of things in a bistro. Some of them are true and some of them aren't." (Alex worked as a fry cook at Bogus Barney's Bistro, a superpopular diner down on 12th and Pacific Coast Highway.)

The phone rang—or rather, it quacked. Alex's phone was shaped like a duck decoy, and it quacked instead of ringing. Alex picked up the mallard and said, "Hello?"

I figured it was Alex's mom, calling to check up on him.

"Oh hi, Janet," Alex said casually. There was a wicked little grin on his face. "Oh yeah, T.J.'s still here. . . . No, he's not taking it well *at all*. In fact, he tried to end his life a few minutes ago by sticking his head in my microwave, but I was able to unplug it before all of his hair fell out."

I threw a couch pillow at Alex, who was laughing silently, but he dodged it.

"No, no, *relax*," he continued. "Of course I'm kidding. Look, do you want to talk to him?"

I was up and pacing now, both thrilled and terrified at the prospect of talking to Janet again. Why'd she call back so soon? Could it be that she'd already changed her mind?

"Oh,". Alex said, with a rare look of surprise. "You want to talk to *me*."

Not knowing what to do, I began to clear the table. Why in the world would Janet want to talk to Alex? I pictured her lying back on her enormous bed, wearing her purple silk nightgown and white slippers, hugging a stuffed animal while she spoke into the phone, and biting her thumbnail while she listened.

The conversation seemed to go on forever. I filled the kitchen sink with hot water. Alex was out of dishwashing liquid, so I had to use shampoo instead. I rattled the silverware so loudly that Alex had to plug one ear with his finger. When the silverware was done, I rattled the pots and made the dishes clatter and squeak. I wanted Janet to know that I was still alive.

I was almost finished when Alex hung up. "Did you remember to use conditioner on the pots?" he joked when he saw the shampoo bottle beside the sink.

"I'm just glad you don't do the shopping at my house, wise man. . . . So, um, what'd she say?" I asked, trying without success to sound cool.

He ran his fingers through his hair and said, "She took a Valium and gradually realized that she was being a fool. You are the man for her and always have been. David Whitworth can take his red BMW and go drive off a cliff, for all she cares. She'll call you just as soon as she's been fitted for a wedding dress. She wants to know how many bridesmaids you'll let her have."

Alex paused to gauge my reaction, which was dead silence, and then said, "Okay. She rambled a bit and seemed a little stressed, but she more or less just called to say that she hoped you and she could still be friends. I'm not making this up—she really said that. She also said it was going to be a 'super year' for the sophomore class. And would we please still come to her end-of-the-summer blowout beach party next weekend."

I liked the first version better.

"If it's any consolation, bud, she asked me about ten times if you were *really* okay," he added.

My spirits began to soar like a rocket. "So you think maybe she's having second thoughts about—"

Alex put his hands up and said, "Whoa! *Down*, boy! I didn't say that at all. I'm just saying that . . . you know, maybe I was a little bit wrong about her."

"A little bit wrong about Janet," I repeated, smiling. "It must've hurt you *a lot* to admit that to me."

He grimaced and said, "I'm in agony here, dude. Don't rub it in."

"You think I should call her?"

"Negative. Give her space."

I didn't much like his answer, but I knew it was good advice. "So what'd you tell her about the party?"

"I told her we'd come," Alex said with the expression of a guy who'd been forced to suck a lemon dry. "You want her back, don't you?"

My pride said no, but my heart said yes. "I don't know what I want," I admitted.

"You and a few billion other people," he said, and we both laughed.

TWO The worst thing about breaking up with someone, especially when it's not your idea, is that you eventually have to explain the mess to *everyone*, including your own family.

Janet had been such a "big catch" that she'd even attracted my father's attention, which was not an easy thing to do. He was an American history professor at a local university—a classic workaholic, absentminded academic. He did honor me at birth, though, by naming me after Thomas Jefferson, his favorite president. I went by "T.J." because I thought it sounded less presumptuous.

"Janet's a lovely, charming girl, son," my dad had told me after I'd had Janet over for dinner with the family. "You can tell a lot about a man by the sort of woman he attracts." Then he'd grinned, patted me on the shoulder, and returned to his study. I was on cloud nine! A compliment like that from my dad was *priceless*.

Now I knew how Cinderella must've felt when her carriage turned back into a pumpkin.

15

After I got dressed, I decided that my best strategy would be to eat breakfast quickly and take off before anyone else got up. Of course, it happened to be the one Saturday my whole family decided to get up early.

I was scarfing down my second bowl of cornflakes and watching a really stupid cartoon when my sister Dana emerged. She was seventeen, two years older than me, and she was a tough act to follow. Ms. Honor Student. Ms. Gifted. Ms. Congenial. She was real pretty, too, when she worked at it. (I, of course, know the secret behind Dana's good looks. If all the guys in the world saw the way she looked on Saturday morning, she'd probably never get a decent date again.)

Dana's first words to me that day were not "Good morning, T.J.," or even, "Turn that TV down, T.J. What're you trying to do, wake up the whole neighborhood?" No, her first words to me were, "Too bad about you and Janet Brooks. I hear she dumped you."

I was so stunned that I spit out a few cornflakes and a banana slice. They formed a perfect right-triangle on my mother's blue-and-white-checkered tablecloth. "How'd you find that out?"

"It's all over town, I'm afraid," she said.

16

"And you'd better wipe that mess off the table before Mom and Dad get up."

"She didn't dump me! She just needs a little space right now, doesn't she, Chester?" I said to the family dog, a good-natured basset hound with ears that could double as stage curtains. Chester was watching TV when I said his name, and looked around to see if this was a drill or the real thing. Chester hated to miss his cartoons. I patted my leg to let him know I really did need him. He stood slowly (Chester did everything slowly, except eat) and wobbled over. He then licked my hand and drooled on my foot, looking up at me with his big, sad, red-rimmed eyes. Chester was a great dog.

Dana gave me a sympathetic, condescending, older-sister look. "A *mutual* decision? That's not what I heard, bro'. But don't take it so hard. She left you for David Whitworth, and he's a first-class jerk if there ever was one." She smiled at me.

So Dana thought David Whitworth was a jerk? They were both seniors this year, so she'd known him for a long time. She'd practically qualify as an expert witness in court, if only there were a way to bring this sort of thing to trial.

"So why'd he go after a sophomore?" I asked.

"He'll pick any rose in the garden, regardless of its age. Poor Janet's in for a bumpy ride, I'll tell you that. David's getting more stuck-up all the time. I wouldn't be surprised if he invited *himself* to the prom this year."

I laughed and started to feel a little more hopeful about getting Janet back. "Just one more week of summer, Dana. Are you ready to be a senior?"

She tossed her hair back dramatically and struck a pose. "Honey, give me an hour in the bathroom and I'm ready for *anything*."

"You didn't tell anyone else in the family about Janet and me, did you?"

She shook her head. "They're all clueless, so far as I know. But they'll figure it out eventually."

Mom emerged next, and her first word was "coffee." We were pretty sure, though Grandma wouldn't comment one way or another, that it was the first word Mom ever spoke. Mom went straight for the coffeemaker, which she programmed each night before she went to bed, and poured herself a cup. "*Aaahhh*," she said. Her posture improved almost immediately, color came back

18

to her cheeks, her short brown hair went from limp to manageable, and even the wrinkles seemed to disappear from her red-and-white-striped nightgown. It was only then that she noticed there were other people up and around.

Dana was eating half a grapefruit for breakfast. I didn't know how she could stand the taste, but she didn't so much as blink when she spooned the fruit into her mouth. I'd tried dumping a cup of sugar on some grapefruit once and still found it impossible to eat. Of course, Dana'd had years of practice. Like a lot of the girls I knew, she'd been on a diet since kindergarten.

"Janet was such a nice girl to have around here, T.J. I'm so sorry," my mother said.

What?! Had my mom just said what I thought she just said? Maybe I was still asleep and this was all a nightmare. I would wake up, get dressed, and sneak out the back door, skipping breakfast altogether. But then I looked down into my bowl and noticed that my cornflakes were wilted and soggy. That sort of detail never showed up in my dreams.

"How'd you know about that, Mom?" I asked incredulously.

"Oh, these things get around," she said casually, lifting a second cup of coffee to her lips. She took a sip and added, "Why she'd let a nice boy like you go in favor of that David Whitworth, I'm sure I don't know. I thought he gave a terrible speech at the awards assembly last year, and his parents act as if they're too good for everybody in this town. Of course, nobody asked for *my* opinion." Nobody *ever* had to ask my mom for her opinion.

"She didn't 'let me go,' Mom. I wasn't her employee. She just needs a little time to herself right now, that's all."

"Well of course she does, dear," my mother said, giving my older sister a meaningful look. This was *killing* me.

When my doe-eyed eight-year-old sister Gretchen appeared in her Disneyland night-shirt and insisted on changing the TV channel, I didn't resist. I was afraid to start a conversation with her. But my caution was useless. Gretchen went into the kitchen and whispered to my mother, "T.J.'s all moody this morning 'cause Janet dumped him yesterday. Can I please have a doughnut wif breakfast?"

"Let's not talk about your brother's personal problems," my mother whispered back.

"And no, you had a doughnut with yesterday's breakfast."

I was about to drown myself in what was left of the milk in my cereal bowl when my father came out of his bedroom with a newspaper in one hand and a pipe in the other. He was always professorial and well groomed, even in his blue bathrobe on a Saturday morning. He looked sort of like Harrison Ford but was genuinely bewildered when other people made the comparison. He didn't see many movies.

I stood up, ready to take it this time. "Okay, Dad, I admit it. She dumped me. It's all over town. Can I go to the marina now?" I pleaded.

My father regarded me with a sharp, puzzled look and then turned to my mother. "Is he taking his medication, Karen?"

"No, it's *Gretchen* who takes the medication, Derek. You go ahead, T.J. I'll explain everything to your father," my mother assured me. The four of them looked at me as I walked to the front door, a pajama-clad jury gawking at another victim of love.

I decided not to tell them that I was planning to sail off to Antarctica and that I didn't expect to see them for at least a decade. Maybe

I'd drop them a note in a bottle as I passed Tierra del Fuego.

I worked at the Long Beach Marina on Alamitos Bay during the summer, doing detail work on sailboats and powerboats. The work was hot and monotonous at times, and some of the boat owners bugged me with their white-glove routines, but it paid pretty well and I got to be my own boss.

On Saturdays I came down to sail, though, not to work—and this Saturday was looking pretty good, weather-wise. The morning haze had burned off to reveal a day that was not too hot and not too smoggy. I had some time to kill before a decent breeze would kick in from the west, so I decided to polish the hull of my dinghy. (My dinghy was basically just a ten-foot-long rowboat that had a hole near the bow for a mast. Not exactly a *yacht*, but it was all mine.)

Janet had liked sailing, I remembered as I poured some polish onto a rag. "You look so handsome and you seem so sure of yourself when you're out on a boat," she'd told me.

I began smearing polish on the yellow hull in broad, circular strokes. When I was honest with myself, I had to admit that sailing would never really be a *passion* for Janet. She mainly saw it as a tanning opportunity, which was sort of like going to the movies because you had a thing for popcorn. And when she was lying out in her bikini, she attracted so much attention from guys on other boats that she could've easily qualified as a hazard to navigation. Still, I'd really gotten a kick out of all the jealous looks those same guys gave *me*.

Polishing the hull began to go more quickly as I imagined that I was rubbing out David Whitworth's perfect, smiling face. Soon my dinghy positively gleamed in the morning sun.

"Nice work," a familiar voice said.

Startled, I looked up into the face of Vivian Chandler. I'd known Vivian since grade school—she was a marina rat, just like me. Her parents had met my parents at the Westport Beach Yacht Club when the two of us were maybe six years old, and they'd hit it off so well that our families started to meet at Catalina Island every summer for a week or two of swimming, snorkeling, sunbathing, and anything else that we could think of. (We didn't take the family sailboat, *Old Ironsides*,

23

out much anymore, though. Dad and Mom and Dana were all too busy these days, not to mention Gretchen.)

"Hi, Vivian. What's shakin'?"

"The whole damn dock, T.J. You're polishing that hull as if you hoped there was a genie trapped inside."

"I could really use a genie right now," I said, almost to myself.

"Yeah, I heard on the radio about you and Janet breaking up. I'm really sorry," Vivian said.

I was shocked. "It was on the ra—" I began but stopped myself, feeling my face redden with embarrassment.

Vivian's laughter gave way to a look of concern and she said, "Hey, I'm *sorry*. God, I don't think I've ever seen you blush before." She crouched next to me and put one hand on my shoulder. "You really *love* her, huh?"

I nodded.

Vivian sat down on the dock, pulled her knees up under her chin, and said, *"Amazing,"* as if she'd just discovered that unicorns weren't imaginary. She was wearing navy blue shorts and a blue bikini top, which she filled out nicely. A straw hat with a blue bow covered her long, very dark brown hair, which was braided in back. I began to smile again when I noticed her earrings: a matching pair of brass Frankenstein heads. (Vivian was the kind of person who would've seen Frank as a misunderstood nonconformist.)

"Aren't you and Paul Walker still together?" I asked. (Paul was a space cadet who styled his ash blond hair with a razor blade and made a small fortune at the high school by stenciling visions of doomsday on student T-shirts.)

"No, I don't think so. It turns out *this* was all he really wanted," she said, gesturing at her fine body. "So two weeks ago I told him to take a hike. He still calls me a couple of times a day to whine about how much he misses me, but I tell him that all he really needs to make himself happy is an inflatable doll and some mood music."

"You're *brutal*, Vivian!"

She shrugged and said, "The truth is not always pretty, T.J., but it beats the hell out of the alternative." She motioned toward the dinghy and asked, "You want some help getting this barge set up?"

I stood up to look out on the bay. The small, isolated patches of wind-rippled water I'd seen earlier in the morning had grown larger and merged with each other. The flags flying over the harbor patrol station were showing distinct signs of life. "I'd love some help," I said as I put the rags and polish back into the dock box. "You want to come along? I'd also love some company."

"Can't," she said, looking disappointed. "Taking the stepmother out for a sail today. I promised Dad I'd be a good girl and help show her the ropes. She's a sweet little thing and all, but most of the time I feel more like her older sister than her stepdaughter. My dad's going to scream for me when they're ready to shove off."

We carried the dinghy to the edge of the dock and slid it into the water. Vivian tied the dinghy off to a cleat while I laid the mast out on the dock and began to rig it. "Can I ask you a personal question, Viv?" I said as I clipped a rope to the boom.

"Give me a *break*, T.J. You can ask me anything. We've seen each other in the buff, remember? I don't care if we were only nine at the time, that *means* something." (We'd once stripped for each other in a cave at Catalina, on a mutual dare, and then laughed ourselves sick.)

"How'd you decide, when your parents

divorced last year, which one to stay with? I mean, why'd you pick your dad over your mom?"

Vivian was in the dinghy now, sliding the rudder into place. "You know, *everybody* asks me that—like I just flipped a coin or something." She looked up and glared at me as I hitched the sail to the mast. "You knew my mom. She was always real *patient* with me, but there were times when you could tell she thought maybe she'd brought the wrong baby home from the hospital. I think she had an old-fashioned idea of a daughter being someone who wears lacy dresses and slaves over piano lessons, not someone who listens to hard rock and decorates her fingernails with rainbows. She used to blame my dad for how I turned out, but I *thank* him for it."

I bundled up the mast and carried it over to the dinghy, and Vivian helped me guide it into its slot. "So you and your dad are like buddies, huh?" I asked after the mast was up.

"Yeah, when we're not fighting like wildcats," Vivian said with a laugh.

"That's *great*," I said enviously.

"Dr. Derek still off in his own little world?" Vivian asked with a smile. "Your father *kills* me." Vivian used to call my dad

"Dream Weaver" because he'd get so lost in thought when he was driving that he could never stay in a lane.

"*Viv-i-an!*" a voice roared from deep within the forest of masts.

"*Com-ing!*" Vivian screamed back, though she made no effort to get out of the dinghy. She smiled up at me and said with an aristocratic accent, "Look, precious, I've gotten rathah comfortable in heah. Would you mind giving me a lift? I'm on your way, you know, just a few gangways ovah. And I'd be *fohevah* in your debt."

"Think nothing of it, madam," I replied as I alighted from the dock into the dinghy and then cast us off.

We scooted out toward the open channel in a freshening breeze, the newly polished hull gliding through the water like a dolphin. Vivian lay her head back on a cushion and closed her eyes. Loose strands of hair danced in the breeze, and a grin dimpled her cheeks. She sure didn't look like a tomboy anymore. She asked how Alex was doing, and after I told her, she smiled, hugged herself, and said, "You know, I really love those little blue glasses he wears. I get hot and bothered just *thinking* about them."

28

"He's available," I said, a little too eagerly, but Vivian just smiled in a shy, self-conscious way and shook her head. Maybe Paul Walker still had his foot in her door, after all.

We cleared the sabot dock and passed the Sea Scout base, and then we made a sharp turn and eased out the mainsail so we could head for the gangway where the Chandlers kept their boat. "I need your advice, Viv," I said. "What would you do if you'd been an outsider all your life, and then suddenly you wanted to change, you *needed* to change, so that you could—" I fumbled for the right words.

"Be in with the *in* crowd?" she suggested as she gave me a dark look and straightened the straps of her bikini top.

"Well, yeah. Although it sounds kind of lame when you put it that way. . . ."

"Doesn't it, though?"

A long torturous stretch of silence followed, which I filled by gazing at gliding sea gulls, floating beer cans, diving pelicans, smoking power-cruisers, graceful sailboats, and low-flying airplanes—absolutely anything but Vivian's disappointed eyes.

The Chandlers' sailboat finally came into view, and Vivian turned to wave cheerfully at her shouting father. She turned back to me and said, "Okay, it's your love life, so here's my advice. My dad told me once, after we moved to a new neighborhood and I was all depressed about being treated like a reject: 'If you can't get invited to any parties, throw one of your own.' So I put up flyers all around the block that advertised an afternoon of free lemonade, ice cream, chocolate-chip cookies, and *fun*. And you know what? It *worked*. Some of the friends I made at that party are *still* my friends."

She couldn't be serious. "You think I should throw a *cookie* party?"

"Don't be stupid, T.J. Stupid people annoy the hell out of me. Use your imagination. Start a club or something. If you can sell Janet Brooks to the masses, you can sell anything."

"Hey, Janet's not so—"

"Vivian! What took you so long?!" her father yelled as we approached the stern of his boat. It was a thirty-four-foot sloop called *Nervous Breakdown*, and its owner appeared, as usual, to be on the verge of one. Roy Chandler was a cheerful, booming-voiced, slap-on-the-back type who seemed to enjoy living on the edge of hysteria. With his big, searching eyes, prematurely graying hair, drooping mustache, and ample beer belly, he looked like a frantic walrus who could never find a large enough rock to rest on.

"Pump your brakes, Dad," Vivian said nonchalantly as we rounded up into the wind and came to a stop at dockside. "I was just helping T.J. here patch up his love life."

Roy stepped off his boat and onto the dock to help his daughter out of the dinghy. He then shook my hand with a bone-crushing grip and said, "My God, Tommy, you sure turned out handsome. It's a miracle! Before you got braces, your teeth entered a room about five minutes before you did!" He laughed louder than anybody else at his own joke and then introduced me to his new wife, a young, pretty, frightened-looking honey-blond named Marcie. She was about a foot shorter than Roy, and when I shook her hand it felt as fragile as spun glass. If he slapped *her* on the back, she'd probably land in San Francisco.

Roy asked all about my parents and Dana and Gretchen, and he wanted to know why they were never around at the yacht club or marina anymore. I told him how busy they were, and he ribbed me good-naturedly about being trapped in a family of overachievers.

31

Marcie stayed close at Roy's side while we talked, and every now and then she snuck a nervous, longing glance at Vivian. My heart went out to Marcie because I had no trouble imagining how tough Vivian would be on a stepmother. Vivian could be tough on *anyone*.

Three

After leaving the Chandlers' boat, I had to tack back and forth into the wind several times to get back up to the Sea Scout base, and then I had to pump my rudder to pass through the dark, windless cavern created by the Second Street bridge. I saw two crabs locking pincers near the bottom of one of the concrete columns that supported the bridge, and the sight made me wonder what Janet was doing. Was she feeling blue? Did she miss me?

She *did* miss me. I was sure of it. Love wasn't an emotion you could just flip on and off like a light switch. So why'd she dump me, then? Was it peer pressure? Janet was a much better person than either Alex or Vivian realized, but she did have at least one major weakness: She was obsessed with what other people thought about her. And I do mean *obsessed*. If someone looked cross-eyed at one of her outfits, the next day it would be on its way to the Salvation Army. If she heard people whispering when she entered a room, she was sure they were whispering about *her*.

I figured maybe her extreme insecurity came from growing up lonely or from "blossoming" late. (She'd told me she was still so flat-chested as an eighth-grader that some creeps had nicknamed her "Janet Wallpaper.")

After the Big Wave Dave campaign, when I became notorious and Janet first really started talking to me, she said, "I envy you, T.J. You never seem to care what other people are saying about you. I mean, you just speak your mind, do what you want to do, and figure to hell with the consequences. I'd *love* to be like that, even for *one day*."

She was romanticizing a little. I mean, half the people I knew threw names at me like "smart ass," "jerk," "creep," "dweeb," and "inveterate trouble-monger." (That last one was used mainly by Phelps, the dean of discipline.) Being a constant target could really *hurt*, no kidding. But hey, I didn't mind Janet romanticizing about me. The truth was, I'd sort of had a crush on her even before she gained a few cup sizes. I think I was taken in by those big, vulnerable blue eyes and the way her knees shook the first time she had to get up in front of the eighth grade drama club and do some Lady Macbeth: " 'Out,' um, 'damned spot.' Ummm, y-you know, '*Out*, I say.' "

I put those memories aside for a second when I reached the Marine Stadium buoy barrier, behind which some water skiers were carving out huge plumes of spray. I decided to hang a left and circumnavigate Naples Island, the man-made island surrounded by Alamitos Bay. That would give me a lot more time to think, which was what I desperately needed to do.

As I tacked back and forth between the sun-kissed luxury homes lining the channel, I thought about the second half of last year, when Janet's blooming good looks and growing self-confidence began to attract hordes of new "friends." She went from being a wealthy nerd to an A-list party guest in about as much time as it takes to slip into a pair of tight designer jeans and say, "Like, where have you been *hiding* yourself? I am *so* jealous of your hair! Let's do lunch and bond for life, ah-kay?" Janet was practically drafted by her new friends to run for sophomore class president, but when Chuck MacQuarrie began to grind her up like so much raw hamburger, those same friends got, like, *really* freaked by his rudeness and were clueless about how to counteract this *retro politico*. Enter yours truly.

When Janet won by a wide margin, her friends patted me on the back but then tried to toss me out with the campaign posters. Janet had to make it clear to them that her interest in me was more than just, shall we say, professional. I was part of the package, and everyone was just going to have to deal with it. Janet stood up for me when she could have just as easily brushed me aside and said, "*Hasta la vista*, sucker!"

I didn't kid myself. I knew her friends were only tolerating me. I was introduced to painful, complex hand-shaking rituals by star athletes. Leadership types asked me for tips on how to sway high school public opinion. I went to parties where I overheard exchanges like:

"Isn't he the geek that almost got that fake surfer elected?"

"Yeah, but Janet's *really* into him, heavy duty. And it's not like he's bad-looking or anything. We're not talking polluted gene pool here. I mean, his sister Dana has a *great* body, and I hear his dad looks *just* like Harrison Ford."

I learned quickly that these popular types

danced on a crowded tightrope and that it was easy for any of them to fall off—if they didn't get knocked off *first*. As far as I could tell, you were dead meat if your teeth began to yellow, your face suffered a major breakout, you were found doing homework on weekends, or if, God forbid, someone could produce solid evidence that you'd shopped at a discount store. But these were the people Janet wanted to hang out with, and the thing I wanted most in the world was to be with Janet, so I also had to deal with her crowd. I actually started to feel like I was becoming part of the group. It was a pretty heady feeling, too, although I'd *never* admit that to Alex.

But now I was on the outside again!

A mother duck swam by, followed by five baby ducks. Leadership? Should I try to get on the leadership council? No way. Even if I wanted to, the next elections weren't until spring. And I was, to say the least, not nearly as popular as Janet.

Should I get another girlfriend and try to make Janet jealous? Swell idea in the movies and on TV, but this was real life. Even if I found a willing girl, I knew I couldn't play with someone's emotions that way, no matter what was at stake.

Sails were going up all over the bay, and people in power boats were revving their engines. Sun worshipers were beginning to lie out on the decks of their waterfront homes, and a little girl with a red-plastic sand bucket was laughing with delight as she was chased by a little boy with a blue plastic sand shovel. "Give . . . it . . . *baaack!*" he was screaming, but anyone could see that he didn't have a chance.

I had to lower my mast to pass under the next bridge. I used an oar for propulsion this time because the breeze had really picked up and the current flowing against me was stronger now. As I passed under the bridge, the rumble of cars, trucks, and buses driving only a foot above my head spooked me a little bit. I sort of expected an earthquake at times like this. Actually, if you lived in California, earthquakes were always rumbling around in the back of your mind somewhere. I could just see the tabloid headlines: EARTHQUAKE PLUS BRIDGE BREAK EQUALS TEEN PANCAKE! or TEEN MEETS MAKER IN SURPRISE EARTH SHAKER! Janet would come to my funeral and cry hysterically and be sorry she'd broken up with me. Alex would eat a quart of ice cream in my honor and then bronze my half of the couch. My mother and sisters would wear black for a few days, and then gut and redecorate my room. My father, totally oblivious to my untimely demise, would eventually commend my mother for her diligence in bringing down the monthly food bill.

As I came out from under the bridge and restepped the mast, I noticed that classes were beginning at the Leeway Sailing Club and that one dinghy had already capsized. The bedraggled captain, who was probably eight or nine years old, clung desperately to his hull, looking awkward and extremely embarrassed in his orange Coast Guard–approved life jacket. It probably didn't fit him right—I'd never found one that did. I smiled as the memories came flooding back, particularly of the sailing classes I'd taken with Vivian. She once rammed a guy with her dinghy because he wouldn't, after several loud warnings, yield her the right of way. He had been knocked overboard, and his dinghy nearly sank. The teacher really tore into Vivian after the victim was rescued, but Vivian just whipped out a rule book, flipped to the section entitled "Rules of the Road: Right of Way and Sound Signals," and started reading aloud. The teacher backed down a little and grumbled something about never insisting on the right of way, but after that incident everybody gave Vivian plenty of sea room.

Vivian's advice about starting a club, which had seemed so stupid to me at first, was starting to make more sense, precisely because it had come from "Take-No-Prisoners" Chandler.

Back when Janet and I were planning campaign strategy and we decided to push for more school involvement in the community, we were thinking in terms of helping the already-existing service clubs to become more active. But why not start a *new* service club to take up new causes? A new club, if it were promoted in the right way, might actually haul in a few hard-to-reach students who would never *dream* of trying to join the upscale, cliquish Sea Lions' League or Keystone Club.

Pulling in the high school fringe groups and putting them to work on worthy causes —that would be *constructive*, wouldn't it? And if I really made a success of the club, made it something so popular and exciting that even Janet couldn't ignore it, then maybe, just maybe, she'd reconsider. . . . Whoa! It was *way* too soon to think that far ahead.

But I was already starting to feel better about life.

I came up with a name for my club a little while later when a man with spiked purple hair and rainbow-colored sunglasses paddled by me on a surfboard. A poodle, sporting a matching pair of sunglasses, was riding on the board with him. "Radical day," the man said to me.

"Totally," I agreed.

The man reminded me of something I'd learned during the Big Wave Dave campaign, which is that surfers have a *very* cool way of looking at life. Their laid-back, semiconscious state of mind seems to spring from a simple philosophy, which I summed up in Big Wave Dave's main campaign slogan: Don't Fight It—Ride It. This philosophy made perfect sense for surfers because they knew that *nobody* could win a fight with the ocean. When a mountainous wave came barreling your way, you either psyched yourself *out*, bailed like a wuss, and paddled for the high ground or you psyched yourself *up*, paddled out to the wave, and made that puppy your *own*. All good surfers knew how to sneak up on the big green monster and trick it into giving up a one-of-a-kind joyride. Only bogus surfers, the weenies who cried with empathy whenever they saw laundry trapped in a spin cycle, were crazy enough to try to meet the monster head-on.

And while I, for sure, had no chance of competing head-on against a wealthy power-tripper like David Whitworth, I knew I could have a lot of fun with the club I'd decided to name the Radical Wave. And if things went the way I hoped, I might just be able to sneak up on that smug ego-with-limbs and relieve him of Janet. Yes! It could happen! After all, Big Wave Dave'd been imaginary, and look how well *he'd* done.

I spent the next hour in a pumped-up state of euphoria, sailing around the rest of Alamitos Bay as I thought of various strategies for the coming semester.

I needed a cause to launch the club with, of course, and I was having trouble coming up with one until I remembered that Grandma and Grandpa Hensley (my mother's parents) had mentioned to me just a few weeks ago that their senior center was running out of funds for its new recreation room. The room was basically finished, but there was nothing to put into it. Helping my own grandparents was a cause I could *really* get behind!

I went to my grandparents' house straight from the marina because I really wanted to nail down this senior center thing. (I had to stay as busy as possible until I saw Janet again or I'd go stark raving mad.) They lived in a tan stucco bungalow near the corner of 15th and Electric, about two blocks from the beach.

My grandma opened the front door and said, "T.J.! What a pleasant surprise!" as if she hadn't seen me in ages, instead of just a week ago. She always welcomed me that way. She looked a lot younger than her seventy-one years. She had only a light dusting of gray in her dark brown hair, and she still had the sparkling, all-seeing eyes of a veteran elementary school teacher, even though she'd retired a long time ago. I came inside and hugged her close. She smelled, as always, like a lemon grove. "I hear your young lady left you," she said gently.

"I'll get her back," I declared.

Grandma gave me a sympathetic look and said, "Would you like some raisins?"

I laughed. I'd been *crazy* about raisins as

a little kid. There were never enough around. "No thanks, Grandma. I take drugs now."

She scowled and slapped me on the butt. "Over my dead body," she said sternly.

"Is that T.J. I hear?" Grandpa's voice inquired from the living room. "Broken any laws yet, boy?"

"Not yet, Grandpa," I said as Grandma and I entered the living room. Grandpa thought that teenagers spent most of their time breaking laws and the rest of their time having—

"Do you know all about condoms, boy?"

And the rest of their time having sex.

"If the need arises, Grandpa," I said. He laughed like a madman. He *loved* that joke.

"Knock it off, you two," Grandma said.

"She'll keep us in at recess," Grandpa said, and then he started howling again. He was a retired elementary school principal, although you could never tell it by looking at him. He was a tall, skinny, white-haired guy with mischievous blue-green eyes and a face deeply etched with laugh lines. He wore plaid pants, a white T-shirt, and tan moccasins. You *might* peg him as the caretaker of a rest home for stand-up comedians, but you'd never, ever believe that he'd held down a suit-and-tie job.

My grandparents' living room, like the rest of their house, was warm, bright, and welcoming. There were lots of creeping plants to touch, interesting pictures to gaze at, and terrific books to read. In other words, it was a second grade classroom without the desks. Grandma brought out a plate of chocolate-chip cookies, and she and I each enjoyed a glass of lemonade while Grandpa guzzled down a beer. We talked about the family for a while, and then I told them all about my plans for the Radical Wave. Grandma got all excited. "That's wonderful, T.J.!" she exclaimed. "I can't begin to tell you how much that would mean to the center. The city has cut our budget to the bone." She talked about all the equipment they hoped to buy, everything from pool tables to exercise bikes. She was jazzed, and I felt great.

"I don't know," Grandpa said skeptically as he stroked the gray stubble on his chin. "The Radical Wave. It sounds sort of like a bug spray."

"Grandpa," I explained as I tried not to laugh, "most high school students go through each day in a coma. If you want to get their attention, you have to be *outrageous*."

Grandpa mulled that over for a minute,

then reached over and slapped me on the shoulder. "You're just the man to do it!" he declared. By this point, I was flying as high as a kite.

We moved on to other topics, but my thoughts stayed on the Wave. With my grandparents eagerly lined up behind the idea, I was sure it would succeed.

Four A week had passed since Janet had given me the bad news. I'd successfully resisted a raging urge to call her by working feverishly to lay the groundwork for my new club. And now it was showtime.

"I'm only wearing this stuff because I like your grandparents," Alex told me as he gazed doubtfully at his Wave uniform.

"I owe you big time," I admitted as we finished up the black-cherry ice cream we were having as a pre-party appetizer.

We left his trailer wearing matching aquamarine canvas shorts, Ensenada beach sandals, and red custom-made T-shirts that showed a guy and a girl surfing down the face of a monster wave. Instead of surfboards, they were each standing on what appeared to be the Westport High bell tower. A slogan beneath the graphic read: CATCH THE RADICAL WAVE! We were also wearing sunglasses with blue neon frames and rainbow-tinted lenses.

Janet lived in a palatial beach house down on Third at Ocean. I'd never determined its

47

square footage because Janet always freaked out when I tried to measure the place, but let's just say you could stuff two or three typical ranch houses into it and still have room for dancing. It stood three stories high, with balconies on three sides, and the back of the house, which faced the ocean, had a wall built entirely out of tinted glass. The other three sides of this monument to wealth and good taste were coated with a stucco so blindingly white that it was almost impossible to look at the house without sunglasses, even at night. Inside this beach mansion was a seemingly endless array of marble surfaces, brass and gold fixtures, teak trims, fine jades, and crystals—all of it protected by a security system that would've stymied James Bond.

Janet's dad was a corporate lawyer, and her mom was an investment counselor. Her parents didn't see much of each other, or of their daughter, for that matter, but when the three of them did get together they enjoyed a first-class home environment.

Janet was greeting people at the door, and there was already quite a crowd. Her long blond hair flowed over a sleeveless peach blouse, and she was wearing white short-shorts that showed off her great legs. Her eyes looked as blue as the ocean and just as inviting. "If I could kiss her just *once*," I told myself, "David Whitworth's spell would be broken and she'd be mine again." (It was easy to believe this kind of stuff when you grew up so close to Disneyland.)

Janet didn't recognize Alex and me at first, so we removed our sunglasses. "Oh my God," she said, "it's you guys!" She laughed, but then she studied my costume more closely and started to look a little concerned.

"Is there anything wrong?" I asked.

"What are you up to, T.J.?"

"Don't panic," I told her. "I'm just following up on your campaign advice by starting a service club. You know, something constructive."

For a split second she looked hurt. "Why, um, haven't you called me?" she asked uncertainly as she continued to study my shirt.

"Called you?" I said as Alex and I exchanged a surprised look. Was I getting mixed signals here or had my romantic radar gone completely haywire?

David Whitworth showed up at that moment, as if on cue. He must've been watching from a distance and decided that Janet was showing a little too much interest in this particular guest. At first glance, David was so good looking it was ridiculous. He was blond, blue eyed, square jawed, lean, tall, and tan—and he had a smile that could sell ice to Eskimos. But if you watched him long enough, you'd notice that there was a cold, vacant look in his eyes, and after a while you might even discover that his smile was a bit frayed around the edges. (My mom had told me when I was a little kid that God had a funny way of making us all a little incomplete, and I was just starting to figure out what she meant.)

At David's side was Mike Geier, one of those pathetic, forever-loyal types who stick to powerful people the way a remora clings to a shark. I'd heard through the rumor mill that Mike would do just about anything for David—like sabotage the campaigns of political opponents, take soiled suits to the dry cleaner, give the Beemer a wax job, and deliver the bad news to discarded girlfriends. He was *that* kind of loyal.

Mike, who basically looked like a bad photocopy of his hero, had been rewarded for his faithful service with a coveted position on the Student Leadership Council. As student body president, David Whitworth had the power to appoint several student commissioners. These appointments, as a courtesy to the president, were usually rubber-stamped by the other elected members of the council. And that's exactly what happened in old Mike's case, even though appointing *him* commissioner of education was like making Al Capone a police chief.

"Well," Whitworth said as he looked at Alex and me, "I didn't know this was a *costume* party. What are you two boys coming as? Surf nerds from outer space?"

Mike practically laughed himself into a coma. Janet tittered without much enthusiasm and then glanced expectantly at me. I was usually the comeback king, but my mind was a blank. I was just stunned, I guess, that Janet had actually chosen this bozo over me. It was *sooo* depressing. . . .

"Costumes *are* fun, aren't they?" Alex said, grinning like a used-car salesman. "And since you've come disguised as a black hole, Dave, we'll play along by staying as far away from you as possible." Alex was great!

A crease made a brief appearance on David's forehead, and Mike took a threatening step toward Alex. "Now what is *that* supposed to mean?" David asked Alex.

I jumped in at this point and said, "A black

51

hole is a mass so dense that it sucks in every-thing around it and emits no light. But hey, Dave, this is a party, not a science class. If you have any more questions like that, you just write them down and save them for Monday. *We're* here to have fun.''

David started for my throat, but Janet stepped between us and said to her new boy-friend, "Is this really the kind of impression you want to make tonight?"

David looked around at the crowd and remembered who he was. "No, Peaches," he said with a loving smile, "I guess not." *Peaches?* I suddenly wished he *had* grabbed my throat and started a knock-down, drag-out fight. I'd have gotten the worst of it, for sure, but *anything* would've been better than hearing him call Janet "Peaches" and then seeing her blush and smile in response.

She turned to me and said almost in a whis-per, "I'll talk to you later, T.J. Please don't leave the party before we have a chance to talk." She gently squeezed my hand.

I nodded as I tried not to notice the smirk on Alex's face.

"You're here for your grandparents, too, bud," Alex reminded me as he led me over to the buffet table. I nodded again. Peaches.

Peaches and cream. The natural color of Janet's skin. How much of Janet's skin had David seen, anyway? Or touched?

I turned and started back toward the front door. I had to kill him—*now*!

"Get a grip, T.J.," Alex said as he came up from behind me and locked his arms around my body. "He's easily twice as strong as you," he whispered. "Don't be a bozo—use your brains!"

"Who're you calling a bozo?" I asked indignantly as I shook him off. But Alex just smiled patiently and led me back to the buffet table. Actually, maybe food wasn't such a bad idea. If nothing else, I could stuff myself and then throw up all over David's polo shirt.

The buffet table was loaded. There was a huge assortment of hot meats, cold meats, finger foods, chips, dips, salads, desserts, and sodas. Janet had spared no expense. (Of course, she didn't have to.) Alex and I stacked our plates as high as we dared and then went to my favorite couch to sit down and pork out. From where we sat you could usually see the cool blue profiles of Catalina Island and the Palos Verdes Peninsula come alive in the rays of the setting sun, but there were too many bodies tonight.

We ate in silence for a while as we checked out our surroundings. In celebration of the school colors, blue and gold balloons and streamers had been hung everywhere—from the marble-mantled fireplace in the living room to the wrought-iron fence that separated the private backyard from the public beach. Lots of people were hanging out in and around the pool and Jacuzzi on the back patio. (It seemed strange to me that anyone would build a pool so close to the Pacific Ocean. Of course, I've always had a distinct preference for seawater over the chlorinated variety.)

The centerpiece of the party was an ice sculpture of a sea lion, the school mascot. Next to the sculpture, red party punch spouted from the blowholes of silver dolphins and cascaded into an enormous open clamshell. (Only Janet could have found a punch bowl like that.) Outfits, indoors and out, ranged from jeans and light sweaters to tube skirts and string bikini tops. Come as you like, the invitation had read. People looked really pumped up, and I couldn't help feeling good for Janet. The party had just started, but you could already tell that it was going to be a major event, the kind of thing people would mark time with later: "Yeah, X happened about a month before Janet Brooks's beach party. . . ."

The only problem with the party was that the guests were so clearly divided into cliques, at least at first, that if a grid had been lowered from the air, no one would have been injured. There were the rah-rahs, the brains, the sci-fi guys, the soshes, the band crowd, the drama kings and queens, the surfers, the future M.B.A.'s, the athletes, the shy crowd, and the burnouts. I was proud that Janet drew support from such a wide constituency. She'd almost certainly be student body president in her senior year—especially with the help of the right campaign manager.

"Okay," Alex said when he'd finished wolfing down his grub, "what's the game plan?"

"The key for tonight is recruitment," I told him. "Before we leave here we have to have as many people interested in the Radical Wave as possible. I'll start with the surfers, and you can work on the athletes."

"Why do I get the athletes?" Alex asked as he wiped mustard off his face with his T-shirt.

"You wear glasses, so they're less likely to smash your face in if you annoy them," I replied.

I approached the surfer crowd casually, anticipating a friendly reception. The surfers had shown a lot of support for Big Wave Dave last year, and I think a few of them still refused to believe that the big guy was just a figment of my twisted imagination. "Hey, 'Spider,' what's happening?" I asked Ricardo Martinez, a guy who'd earned his nickname by consistently staying on his board after everyone else had wiped out.

"Hey, Durant," he replied. I'd gotten to know Spider last spring when I did a special about the surfing team for the school TV news broadcast. It wasn't easy to talk to Spider because he kept most of his face hidden behind a curtain of black hair. He eyed my clothes. "Did you dress in the dark or what?" he asked, and then he laughed. Well, it wasn't actually a laugh. It was more like a cross between a grunt and a yawn, and it lasted about two seconds.

"Doesn't everyone dress in the dark?" I asked.

He surprised me by laughing again, for almost five seconds this time. Such an outburst from Spider was apparently a rare event and it got the attention of a lot of surfers standing nearby.

"Hey, is the Spide buzzed or what?" one of them asked.

"What's this Radical Wave garbage?" Spider asked me.

"A new club. For students who want to help people and who like triple-thick pizza." (I'd settled on triple-thick pizza as a way of luring people to the first meeting. I was sure Vivian'd be pleased.)

Spider began to pull his hair away from his face but then thought better of it. "Are you spun or what?" he asked. "I don't join any bogus clubs. Hell, I've never joined a club in my life. I surf."

I had known Spider would be a hard sell, but he was sort of a hero to the other surfers so I really needed his support. I told him about my plans to help the senior center, and as he listened he actually *did* pull his hair away from his face. (Aside from a minor acne problem, he was not a bad-looking dude.) "*Mi abuelita*, my grandma, she uses that center," Spider said. His dark brown eyes came alive with affection. "She tells me sometimes that I'm a lazy good-for-nothing, that my head is filled *con alga*, with seaweed. But maybe if I do something for this center of hers, she'll get off my case for a while. Do you think?"

57

"She'll *love* you for it," "Sandbar Sam" Utu told Spider. Sam was a Polynesian transplant who surveyed his suburban surroundings with amused brown eyes, expressed his great enthusiasm for life with a glass-shattering laugh, and sported some of the thickest arms ever seen on a high school student. Sam turned to me and said, "This is a good idea, Durant. Ever since I came here as a little kid, I've been mighty pissed off by the way old people are treated. Instead of being honored, they're talked down to like babies. They're tossed away like old newspapers and left to rot on park benches, when they should be the sun their families spin around! You comprehend me, Durant? It's a raw deal! I don't like it!"

I smiled gratefully at Sam. His booming voice had captured the attention of a lot of people, not just the surfers. "I totally agree," I said. "And not only will we help them out, but we can do stuff for ourselves, too, like wipe out all that bogus graffiti down by the pier."

"*Major,*" Sam said, punching me on the shoulder. It was all I could do to remain standing. "I'm in. Where do I get one of those goofy shirts?"

I was hoping someone would ask. "At Pizzaz T-shirts on Main and Central. I'm planning to order them in bulk and sell them to club members and non-club members as a fund-raiser. Could you spread the word, Sam? People seem to listen to you."

Even the muscles on Sam's arms seemed to beam at the compliment. What a salesman he would make!

Spider also committed to the Wave, which inspired most of the rest of the surfers to do the same. Even the holdouts agreed to at least check it out, especially after I promised free pizza at the first meeting and a beach party sometime later in the fall. "Dizzy Danny" Donahue, whose hair was so blond from sun exposure that it'd actually turned white, held back until I explained that the senior center was a gathering place for people older than fifty-five and *not* a hangout for twelfth-graders.

"Too many wipeouts at the wedge," Sandbar Sam said, explaining about Dizzy Danny. I figured Sam knew what he was talking about.

I let the surfers return to their never-ending conversation about wave conditions as I made the first of many trips to the bathroom. (I was incredibly nervous.) As I made my way through the house, I listened to the voices of the party: "Hey, look. There's the creep Janet went out with for almost the entire summer, until she *finally* came to her senses." . . . "Can you even believe what he's wearing? I would be so embarrassed. What a total geek!" . . . "It's just the bitchin'est bootleg CD on the planet, dude." . . . "Come upstairs with me, Jennifer, *please*? All I want to do is kiss, I swear." . . . "Is that Dana Durant's little brother? Oh my God, he's gotten cute! I remember when he used to have, like, really stupid teeth!" . . . "It simply *has* to be Harvard, Yale, or Stanford. Although I suppose I *might* consider Berkeley in a pinch, but only if they *really* want me." . . . "That doesn't taste like punch anymore, Kirk, you sleazebag! What'd you put in it?" . . .

By the time I found Alex, my brain was on overload. "So how's it going?" I asked as I tried to clear my head of static.

"Not well," he replied. "Most of the athletes wouldn't commit to the Wave because they said they were already in 'real' service clubs. I'm pretty sure they meant that as an insult. I got the nod from a few pizza-lovers on the golf team and a 'maybe' from one guy on the soccer team. That was the best I could do."

I laughed. "That's a whole lot better

than nothing. Are you enjoying the party?"

Alex shook his head. "I feel like I'm trapped in a warehouse full of mannequins. The only decent conversation I've had so far was with Robin Frye, and I ran into her by accident."

"Robin Frye? 'The Ice Queen' of algebra II–trig? I didn't think she was allowed to talk to guys until *after* she graduated from medical school."

"She was sitting alone upstairs in the library, reading a book of poetry. You know— Emily Dickinson, T. S. Eliot, Sylvia Plath," Alex said with a look of longing in his eyes. Then he grinned like the Cheshire cat and added, "After all, T.J., you can't judge people strictly by how popular they are."

I knew who he meant.

"Hey, I thought you admitted you were wrong about Janet."

"No," he corrected me, "I admitted that I was a *little bit* wrong about Janet. And that's *all* I admitted."

"So you think I'm wasting my time here?" I asked defensively.

"That depends on what you're here for. Is the Radical Wave really a service club or is it just a get-Janet-back club?"

I thought for a minute. The truth was that my motives for starting the Wave had gotten pretty jumbled. "I'll take the Fifth on that," I finally said.

Alex grinned and said, "Good answer." We exchanged a high-five and then split up to work the crowd some more.

I didn't have much luck recruiting for the Wave among the rah-rahs or the soshes because they seemed to think I was, like, stepping on their turf. The burnouts responded to my spiel with "Whatever," which might or might not be interpreted as a positive response. Alex reported to me later that he had some success with the sci-fi guys, mainly because they thought *The Radical Wave* would make a terrific title for a Star Trek movie. The brains were generally intrigued by the concept of a new service club but chose to delay their commitment until a cost-benefit analysis could be effected. The hard-core nerds were, as usual, more than happy to be asked.

I ran into Vivian as I made the rounds and was surprised to find her hanging out with Ray Webster, a nice, quiet sort of guy who could touch his nose with his tongue. It was rumored, partly because he rarely changed his clothes and partly because he got straight A's in all his classes, that Ray was actually a holographic image being projected from somewhere inside the school science building, a computer-generated curve-breaker meant to serve as an academic inspiration for the rest of us. I didn't put much faith in this rumor, although Ray did seem to fade quite a bit in certain light.

"I didn't expect to see you here tonight," I told Vivian as I hugged her. She was looking delicious in a white peasant blouse, tight-fitting acid-washed blue jeans, and a black Greek fisherman's cap. One of her gold earrings was a question mark, and the other was an exclamation point.

"I didn't expect to see me here either," she said with a shrug. "But Paul and I are absolutely through now, and Ray here sort of caught me on the rebound. He's a real party animal, aren't you, Ray?"

Ray looked bewildered as he scanned his memory banks for the term "party animal." Feeling a little sorry for him, I offered him my hand, and he shook it briskly.

Vivian asked about my Wave uniform, so I told her about the club. "Excellent," she said. "It sounds like you've really got your act together. And hey, if the triple-thick pizza's any good, I may just join up myself."

"Please do," I said. I tried not to stare at her body, but she really looked great.

"If you keep this up," Vivian told me with an amused smile, "I'll have to call the police and have your eyes arrested."

I blushed so deeply that I practically singed my face. Vivian doubled over with laughter.

"I don't understand what's so funny," Ray told Vivian as he vigorously shook his head. He was getting a little frantic.

She pinched his cheek and said, "Don't sweat it, cupcake. It's just a little casual sex between consenting friends."

Ray's eyes began to cross, and he suddenly excused himself and made a beeline for the bathroom (in search of a friendly power outlet, no doubt). Vivian linked her arm through mine, and we walked over to the dolphins for punch refills. "And how goes the campaign to recapture Princess Janet from the evil clutches of Dark Prince Whitworth?" she asked.

"You know," I said, trying not to sound too annoyed, "you and Alex would be perfect for each other."

Vivian sipped some punch, gave me a

searching look, and then said, "That's a damn strange way to answer my question. Although I'm flattered that you'd think of me and Alex together."

"Sure! I think you'd really hit it off. Just go to the library on the second floor, pick out a book of poetry, and then—" I was planning to give her more detailed advice, but at that moment Janet appeared.

"Hi, Vivian," Janet said. "Are you enjoying yourself?"

Vivian's smile thinned out and her eyes darkened as she took Janet's hand and said, "This is a sublime party, Janet. I feel privileged to be here. I'm sure that I will look back on this evening as one of the high points of my young life. I'm *so* indebted to you!" Vivian kissed Janet on the cheek, glared stonily at me, and then sailed briskly away.

"Do you think she meant that?" Janet asked as she touched the cheek Vivian had kissed.

"I wouldn't take her too seriously if I were you," I said. "She and Paul Walker have broken up for good, so her emotions are a little raggedy right now."

"Oh," Janet said, looking away from my raggedy eyes. After a long pause, she came close to me, took my hand, and whispered, "Let's go upstairs and talk."

"That's a *swell* idea," I whispered back.

It took us a while to get upstairs, though, because Janet was stopped by a ton of people along the way and had to take care of a lot of urgent hostessing chores. With my help, she forced six feverish couples out of the enormous closet in the front hallway. Rex Finkelstein had been thrown into the pool with all his clothes on, so Janet loaned him a blowdryer. Esmeralda Hagan was crying because Renee Wurtfell had taken Esmeralda's date, Jorge Ayala, out on the beach for an astronomy lesson. Janet agreed that Renee was a worm and then shepherded Esmeralda over to Anne Winterman for comfort and counseling. Paul Walker, wearing a black T-shirt emblazoned with a color picture of a burned-out rain forest and the slogan HOPE IS DEAD—LONG LIVE DESPAIR, was found in a broom closet near the pantry, toking on a mammoth joint. Despite spirited protests from a gathering crowd of eager spectators, Janet got Paul to extinguish the joint and to toss the remains into the trash compactor; she then gently persuaded him to go home and sleep off his heartbreak. She handled each crisis like a pro. It was hard to believe that she'd ever been shy.

When we finally got up to her bedroom though, she collapsed onto her bed, covered her face with her hands, and said, "God, T.J., now the kitchen smells like a marijuana plantation! What am I going to do?"

I thought for a moment. "Sell tickets?"

We laughed together, and then she sat back up and gestured for me to sit down next to her on the edge of her bed. As I did so, I gazed out through the glass wall at the stars, the necklace of lights on the pier, and the waves gently crashing along the distant shoreline. Nothing had changed, but everything was different. "So what's the scoop, Peaches?" I asked her.

She winced, and her smile shriveled into a frown. "So that's how you're going to act?" she asked.

"Oh, no," I said, putting an innocent hand to my chest. "Did I give the wrong reading? How would you *like* me to act, *Peaches*? Is that what gives David the edge—he acts the way you want him to?"

Janet stood up, and so did I. "Look," she said angrily, "I brought you up here to apologize for the way I broke up with you, okay? It was lousy not telling you about David, and

I admit it. I'm sorry. But I can't take your sarcasm tonight. So if you're just going to lay into me, then I want you to leave—*now*!"

I was stunned. She was so mad that she was shaking. "Tough week at the office, dear?" I ventured.

She tried to maintain her intense anger but gave up and collapsed back onto the bed, covering her head with a pillow. "The *worst*," she mumbled. She tossed the pillow aside and said, "You wouldn't believe how much work it takes to get a party like this rolling. . . . Actually, *you* would." She sat up and said, "I really could've used your help, T.J., especially with the . . ." Her voice trailed off as she remembered our status, and then she started chewing busily on her thumbnail.

I sat down next to her and put an arm around her. She stiffened at first but then relaxed and rested her head against my shoulder. "Just kick back for a few minutes," I whispered, "and then we'll talk." She nodded gratefully and closed her eyes.

I was so jazzed to be holding her this way again that I forced myself not to think too hard about what it might mean or not mean for the future, and instead let my mind wander around her bedroom. The space was a collage of pastel fabrics and leather-bound books; posters of fashion models, movie stars, music stars, and prominent world leaders, past and present; miscellaneous photographs (I noted sadly that most of the ones that included me had already been taken down), paintings, awards, letters, and greeting cards; an exercise bike, a trampoline, a computer station; a large color TV, two VCRs, a top-of-the-line stereo system; and a huge menagerie of stuffed animals. In spite of the major material overkill, I'd spent a lot of happy hours in this room.

Janet stirred after a few minutes and sat back up on the bed. "Thank you," she said as she slowly stroked my shoulder with her fingertips. Our eyes met, and I leaned forward to kiss her. Her lips began to part and her eyes began to close, but then she pushed me away.

"I shouldn't have brought you up here," she said, as much to herself as to me.

"I still love you, Janet."

"Please don't say that, T.J. . . . Look, the high school years are a time for dating lots of people, not a time for tying marriage knots."

I laughed at her, and her eyes flashed with anger. "Come on," I said. "That's so hokey! You sound just like your mother. That woman has never liked me, not since I beat on one of her wigs with a toilet brush. I *swear* it jumped off the counter by itself."

Janet laughed in spite of herself. "What about the time you groomed our hedges to look like the stone heads on Easter Island?"

"That was a hit all over town," I said, glad that Janet was laughing. It really was—a photograph of the Brookses' altered hedges had made it into the *Orange County Times*.

I leaned toward her again. She looked at me uncertainly. "Give me another chance, Janet. I'll make it worth your while."

This time we did kiss, and it was a while before she pushed me away. "T.J.!" she protested. "You're confusing me! I was just trying to set things straight with you, but I should've known better."

"Look," I said, savoring the taste of her kiss, "I don't expect a lifetime commitment here, babe, but I do think we're worth more than just one summer together, you know?"

Janet balled her hands into fists and began rubbing her thighs with them. She only did this when she was majorly stressed. "Things change, T.J.—*people* change. Fast, sometimes. My life is a lot more complicated than it used to be, while yours is . . . Well, it's just difficult for you to understand what I'm going through, that's all."

I looked into one of her full-length mirrors and said, "I sure am pretty when you're mad."

She shook her head and rolled her eyes in exasperation.

"I just want you to keep an open mind about me," I continued. "That's all I'm asking. Give me a chance to prove—"

"Janet?" David Whitworth's voice inquired from the hallway, "*Janet*, are you in there?"

Janet froze, and my heart skipped a few beats. "If David finds us in here together," she whispered shrilly, "he'll freak!"

I suffered a few bleak visions of bloodied noses and missing teeth, but then I chilled out. Use your brains, Alex had said. And he was right. I could get out of this without so much as a scratch if I could just manage to keep the enemy on the defensive. I flashed Janet a peace sign and then went to work.

"Okay, if that's the way it has to be, then I won't stand in your way!" I said in a loud, dramatic voice. "If you really think that David is the father of your unborn child, Janet, then of course you should marry him!"

Janet's eyes widened with shock and she mouthed the word "no" as she shook her head vigorously. "Of course," I continued, "if *I* should turn out to be the father, then I will take full responsi—"

The door burst open and David came charging into the room. "What are you talking about?!" he demanded to know as he clutched at the neck of my T-shirt.

I winked at Janet and then gently removed David's hand from my person. "Classical music, actually. Why do you ask?"

"That's not what you were talking about!" David said menacingly. He tried to look menacing, too, but his carefully groomed features would just not allow it.

"Oh my goodness," I said, looking at Janet. "He's on to us. You don't suppose he was listening in at the door, do you? What do you guess the student body would think of a president who goes around listening in on other people's conversations? I was just reading the other day about this guy named Nixon, and he—"

"Okay, *enough*," Janet said, holding up her hands and fighting back a smile. "You can go now, T.J. I'll explain everything to David."

"Start with the theory of relativity," I suggested. "It's essential for the understanding of black holes."

"Can I kill him?" David asked Janet.

She shook her head. "I doubt it. Anyway, he was just leaving, weren't you, T.J.?"

I nodded, but David grabbed my arm as I turned to go. "And as for your stupid club, Durant, just remember that it has to go through *my* leadership council before it can be chartered on campus. I think it has a very poor chance of ever being approved. Do you get my drift, little man?"

I glared at him and said, "Thank you for speaking so clearly. I took the precaution of concealing a miniature tape recorder in the waistband of my shorts. I can't wait to play your statement to the entire school on the TV news broadcast this Monday."

I was bluffing, of course, but he didn't know it. He chased me all the way down the stairs. When we got to the landing I shouted, "Ladies and gentlemen, a warm round of applause, if you please, for our new student body president—David Whitworth!"

He had to grin and wave as I retreated into the cheering crowd, but there was murder in his eyes.

Five I left home at 6:00 A.M. on the first day of school so I could swing by the trailer park and wake up Alex. He'd worked a double shift on Sunday at Bogus Barney's Bistro, and I figured if I didn't do anything about it, he probably wouldn't get to school until second or third period.

Once Alex was dressed, he and I took off on our bikes to have breakfast at a doughnut shop. (His mom had come home very late the night before and surprised him with a pizza, and he didn't want to disturb her sound sleep.)

"Another year in paradise," Alex said groggily as he tore into a custard bar.

"Who knows?" I said cheerfully, "This might be the year you really fall in love. What do you think of Vivian Chandler, by the way?"

"Vivian? Well, I hadn't really thought. . . . Hey, I gotta show you something!" Alex said excitedly as he unzipped his backpack and began to rummage through it. "I completely forgot!" He was a maniac, suddenly. He un-

74

zipped the pack, pulled out a book, and handed it to me: *The Sonnets of William Shakespeare*.

"I have a copy of this at home. You gave it to me last Christmas," I reminded him.

"It's not for you," he said, grinning a little self-consciously. "It's for Robin Frye. I'm meeting her at lunch today by the tower. She's very enthused about the Wave, by the way. I convinced her it was a really good idea."

Wow! They meet by chance in the library at Janet's house on Friday night, and already he's giving her a book? Of course, people have to meet somewhere, and there are rumors about these rare cases of instant mutual attraction, but I'd thought Alex and Vivian would make such a perfect match, and I knew almost nothing about Robin Frye, except that she was sort of plain, had intimidating ice blue eyes, wore black turtlenecks to school practically every day, imprisoned her blond hair in a bun, and had been at the top of the honor roll since nursery school. . . . On the other hand, she was *heavy, deep, and real*! This was great news! I smiled at Alex, and we slapped a high-five. "You're an animal!" I told him. "What woman can resist *The Sonnets of*

William Shakespeare? Don Juan has *nothing* on you in the romance department. Let's go ravage some more doughnuts—my treat!"

"You're on!" Alex said.

If you had to go to high school, Westport High was not a bad place to suffer through the experience. The auditorium and bell tower had been built in 1908, which in southern California practically qualified as the Stone Age. At first glance, the auditorium building was just another typical beige-stucco-with-red-tile-roof job, but a closer inspection revealed lots of turn-of-the-century roaring lions and screaming gargoyles around the edges. Very cool-looking, especially on foggy mornings and late at night when the creatures seemed to spring to life. The tower was a classic—tall and narrow with a cone-shaped roof and topped with a ball and spire. The bells inside it didn't ring anymore, but the bells were still there, a fact that set the tower apart from some of the fake towers at other high schools.

Unfortunately, the farther you got from the tower on campus, the more modern and ugly Westport High became. It was a budget thing, I suppose, but I thought it was pretty sad that the math-science building had ended up looking like a Marine barracks and that the school cafeteria could easily double as a bomb shelter. (At least they were consistent about the cafeteria—it definitely served the kind of food you'd expect to eat in a bomb shelter.) We also had first-class athletic facilities: a huge gym, pool area, weight room, and large fields for track, football, and baseball. It was all lost on me, though. As far as I was concerned, "P.E." stood for prison environment, a place where you were forced to dress down in smelly rags and allow yourself to be humiliated by hulking thugs with superior eye-to-hand coordination. (Of course, if P.E. meant sailing instead of weight training, things would be different.)

But like I said before, 2,000 teenage Sea Lions could easily find a worse place to wait out their adolescence.

The campus was buzzing with activity when Alex and I arrived, about a half-hour before the first classes would begin. People were comparing class schedules, outfits, shoes, hairstyles, jewelry, and summer vacations.

I was wearing my Radical Wave T-shirt, and it attracted quite a few comments as we walked through the central quad: "Great shirt. Where can I rip one off?" . . . "Durant, you weasel, trying to start a club?" . . . "*Um,* is that, like, the *tower* being used as, like, a *surfboard*?" . . . "Radical Wave? Uh, I don't *think* so." . . . "You know, I think my dad used to be in that Radical Wave party, but I'm pretty sure he votes Republican now."

By the time we got out of the quad and headed across the main campus green to the administration building, I was wondering aloud if the Wave could be sold to the high school masses.

Alex laughed and said, "Scary, isn't it? But the Wave is a great concept, T.J. It'll fly, even at this turkey farm. Who's our advisor, by the way?"

"I'm hoping to get Mr. Horton."

"You mean *Count* Horton? Your drama teacher? The guy who sleeps upside down in the wardrobe closet at night and never appears in sunlight without a trench coat and a hat?"

"Yeah, I know he's a little strange, but he likes me and I know I can trust him to stand up for us if—"

"Does he have tenure? They've been laying teachers off like crazy at this school. It's no good to get an advisor the administration can just boot into the street."

"Alex, Mr. Horton was at Westport High back when people wore *polyester*. I've seen pictures."

"Hmmm. And he still looks so young. I'm going to hang some garlic around my neck when I come to club meetings, just in case."

We picked up our class schedules at the sophomore table in front of the administration building. Alex gazed at his list of classes, sighed with disgust, and said, "High school 'is a tale told by an idiot, full of sound and fury, signifying nothing.' "

"They made a mistake?" I asked.

He nodded. "They put me in sewing instead of sociology. Damn computer's always putting me in home ec classes."

I laughed. "Somebody's obviously trying to tell you something."

"Chill out, Betty Crocker. I'm a domestically responsible guy. In fact, just yesterday I went out and bought some dishwashing liquid for my kitchen staff."

"The kitchen staff thanks you!"

Alex went into the administration building while I strolled across the green and around to the drama classroom at the back of the auditorium building.

I entered the darkened classroom and

found Mr. Horton was sitting at his desk, reading the newspaper by candlelight as he smoked a cigarette. (The entire campus had been designated a no-smoking zone.) "Out until the bell," he said, without looking up. "Stay outside until the bell rings."

I approached his desk and said, "I'm sorry to bother you in the middle of a religious ceremony, sir, but I need a favor."

Mr. Horton looked up sharply. He had a dark goatee and green, catlike eyes, and the flickering candlelight gave him a distinctly sinister look. But then he smiled and said, "A religious ceremony, indeed. T.J., you smart ass, it's good to see you again! I feared you were just another freshman dumped on me by the counseling staff. Have a seat."

I sat down and saw that he was reading the front page of the *Times* and that he'd already written several angry comments in the margins. Same old Horton. "You know," he told me, leaning forward in his intense way as he stabbed the front page with his right index finger, "I've concluded that the world had finally gone mad. Five teenagers were murdered over the weekend. Five! In one weekend! I *weep* for you young people. A couple of million years of evolution, and what do we have to offer our children? Hand-held computer games and drive-by shootings! What the hell kind of outcome is that, I ask you?!" He banged his fist down on the desk, upset the candle, and set the front page on fire.

"It's terrible," I agreed as I quickly helped him smother the flames with the classifieds.

He calmed down as he propped the candle upright again. "The last thing this department needs," he whispered with a grin, "is a visit from the fire marshal. I'd go to prison for the wardrobe closet alone." He took a long drag of his cigarette, until the tip glowed orange like an angry sun. Then he exhaled and said, "Now what can I do for you?"

I told him all about the Wave, how the idea had originated, and how large—or rather, how small—I expected the club to be. As I spoke Mr. Horton got a fond, distant look in his flickering eyes, and when I finished he said in an uncharacteristically subdued voice, "No cause for the good is ever too small, T.J." He crushed his cigarette into the remains of a croissant and continued, "When I was your age, we thought we could save the world by going on peace marches and practicing free love in Golden Gate Park. Now people are marching for safe sex, and you can't find peace anywhere. But there's no point in giving up on trying to save the world because the alternative is . . ." He paused for a moment and then shook his head with disgust. "I've forgotten my next line," he said. (He regularly insisted that the dialogue for his entire life had been scripted for him at birth, and every now and then I got the eerie feeling that he wasn't kidding.) "Anyway, I'll do it. I'll be your advisor. But remember, I'm a slave to my rehearsal schedule. Rehearsals must come first."

"Of course," I said, and then I thanked him profusely. I asked if I could use the classroom after school on Wednesday for an organizational meeting. He said I could, even though he wouldn't be able to attend. He was going to a one-day-only costume sale in West Hollywood that the department literally couldn't afford to miss.

Then he got a puckish look on his face and said, "So where is our beautiful blond Juliet this morning?" Janet and I had played the title roles in the freshman class production of *Romeo and Juliet* last year. "Is it true she'll be forsaking drama for leadership this year?"

"I'm afraid so. And she's not really my Juliet anymore, either. What I mean to say is that we, um, she and I—we're not exactly together anymore, right now, exactly," I said, glad this wasn't an audition.

Mr. Horton lighted up a fresh cigarette and took a long, hungry drag on it. Then he blew out a cloud of smoke that slipped like a phantom into the darkness. " 'So we'll go no more a-roving / So late into the night / Though the heart be still as loving / And the moon be still as bright,' " he said, in a younger voice.

"Lord Byron?" I guessed.

"Jessica Hoffman," he said, looking past me. "She had long, kinky red hair and sparkling emerald eyes that molested the soul. I was living on a commune in Mendocino County that summer, and one warm afternoon as I took a break from my chores I saw her rise like Venus out of a swimming hole."

He cut himself off. I urged him to go on, but he wouldn't. He stood and vigorously shook my hand. "Good luck, T.J.! And please turn on the lights as you leave the room."

I got out of my journalism/TV news class on a pass just before lunch and headed over to the leadership office to get an application to charter the Wave. The leadership office was in a spacious, carpeted, three-room building that had its own Xerox machine and seemingly unlimited supplies. The walls were covered with awards and pictures of students having a great time. The school emblem—an image of the school tower surrounded by sea lions, oil derricks, and palm trees—was painted on the wall behind the council meeting table. It was all very impressive looking.

The leadership advisor, Mr. Ito, had his office in the short hallway adjoining the main meeting and activity area. There was nothing intimidating about Mr. Ito. He was a talkative, friendly guy who had a smile for just about everybody. He hadn't been too hip on the Big Wave Dave thing last fall, I have to admit, but then last spring he'd made a point of complimenting me for the work I'd done on Janet's campaign. He'd actually shaken my hand, in the leadership office, in front of everybody.

The office was swarming with activity as student leaders prepared for lunchtime welcoming and orientation activities. I caught Janet as she was about to leave for the quad. She literally jumped back in surprise when she saw me, then quickly apologized. She was wearing a royal blue blazer with a school pin on the lapel. She'd obviously spent a long time on her makeup, and her hair was pulled back into a neat ponytail. All in all, she looked more like an administrator than a student.

"No need to apologize," I said as my heart started beating like a conga drum. "You look really professional, by the way. That jacket is great. How's everything going?"

"You really like it?" she said eagerly, modeling the blazer for me. "You always said royal blue was my best color, and when I found this at—" she stopped herself, looked around the room, and took in several disapproving stares. She bowed her head, took me by the arm, and guided me outside.

"Spies," she whispered angrily when we stopped, well out of earshot of the students in the leadership office. "It's absolutely disgusting. I'll talk to *whoever* I want, *whenever* I want." She glanced at her gold watch and said, "I've got to run, though, T.J. The bell's going to ring any second now." She withdrew her arm and began to talk to a nearby eucalyptus tree. "We had a great summer together," she said in a voice that suddenly sounded rehearsed, "and I'll always love you for it. But let's not ruin the memory by trying to force things to go on longer than they're meant to, okay?"

The bell rang, and she turned to me. Her face was defiant, but her eyes looked doubtful and sorry.

"My new club is meeting in the drama room on Wednesday after school. Will you come?" I asked.

She seemed surprised by the question, and then relieved. "I'll sure try," she said brightly. "We understand each other, then? About us, I mean." She paused, and then added impulsively, "I know you'll find a new girl to love in no time."

I watched with fascination as her smile collapsed under the weight of her own prediction. She turned abruptly away from me and began to storm off in the direction of the quad, mumbling sullenly about how I'd made her late.

Janet was still confused! I sailed back to the leadership office and picked up an application form from Mr. Ito. He said he thought the club was a "neat idea." As I sat down and filled out the application, I imagined Janet sitting front and center at the first Wave meeting, her eyes shining with love and admiration, her lips mouthing the words, "Please forgive me, darling. It was all a terrible mista—"

"Your Radical Wave sounds radically stupid to me, Durant," Mike Geier said behind my back. "So far I've only seen geeks and losers wearing your T-shirts. What do you think about *that*?"

I turned to face him. I again noticed that he had basically the same generic haircut and cookie-cutter features as his friend David Whitworth. Were these guys turned out in a factory somewhere and then distributed to high schools nationwide? "I don't doubt your ability to recognize a loser when you see one, commissioner," I said calmly, "but don't underestimate the Radical Wave. It might just roll right through this office and carry you out with it."

Geier seemed puzzled. I knew it was unfair to use metaphorical imagery on him when David wasn't around to translate, but I couldn't resist.

I walked over to Mr. Ito and handed him the completed application. He said he'd have an aide take it to Mr. Horton for his signature and then it would be put on the leadership council agenda for approval. I'd be notified of the meeting date.

Mike made a choking gesture as I walked out of the office, but I didn't react. I was going to get the Radical Wave chartered no matter what obstacles he and his fair-haired boss tried to throw in my way. Westport High badly needed a service club for outsiders, a league for the cliqueless and clueless that wouldn't be afraid to take on new causes. And I had to prove to Janet that I was a megaconstructive guy. She wouldn't come back to anyone less.

Six Twenty-three people came to the drama classroom for the first meeting of the Wave, and not one of them was Janet. I was majorly bummed. Maybe somebody had talked her out of it, I reassured myself as I watched Alex and Robin swap love sonnets before the meeting got under way. The small crowd enthusiastically scarfed down the six triple-thick pizzas I'd bought from Pablo's Monster Pizza Emporium.

"Good eats," Vivian told me with a wink. "The word'll get around." She was wearing a brown leather bomber jacket and matching cowboy boots. "My butt-kickin' boots," she said with a smile. They looked great, but whose butt was she planning to kick?

"Triple-thick pizza—I *like* it!" Sandbar Sam said as he slapped me on the back.

"I'm glad," I said, wondering for a moment if he'd turned my spine to powder.

When I could stall no longer on Janet's behalf, I reluctantly walked up to the podium on the small wooden stage and started the meeting. "Good afternoon, and welcome to the first meeting of the Radical Wave," I said as cheerfully as I could.

A few people applauded, and I asked the students who were wearing Radical Wave T-shirts to stand up and show off their club spirit. The pizza had put the crowd in a good mood, and it was my job to harness that enthusiasm. After all, I reminded myself, I was an expert at this sort of thing. I didn't need Janet's help to make this club a success.

"Why does Westport High need yet another service club?" I asked in a more energetic voice. "Because there are so many of us here who're willing and able to serve this school and our community, but we're never invited or allowed to. Why? Maybe it's because we don't wear the right clothes, or know the right people, or have the right parents. Maybe it's because we like to do our own thing and to speak our own minds, and that bothers the powers that be. But we can't let ourselves be intimidated by a clique of insecure bozos who want nothing less than total control over student life at this high school. We only pass through this place once—"

There was a grunt of protest from Dizzy Danny Donahue, followed by widespread laughter.

"—more or less," I continued, provoking still more laughter, "and if we don't stand up for our rights now, we won't get a second chance later. And so we *will* serve, whether they want us to or not." The crowd applauded, and then I talked a bit about the planned fund-raising drive for the Ocean View Senior Center and how it would help out my grandparents and other senior citizens in Westport Beach. Spider and Sam both got up and made their pitches in support of the idea, just like they had at Janet's party.

"We've already started raising a little money by selling T-shirts," I continued. "And I've got some great news! It turns out that Bob Maxwell, of Crazy Bob's Electronic Empire, is a former student of my grandmother's. She got him to agree to donate some VCRs to our cause so that we can raise some serious money by selling raffle tickets." (I had cracked up when Grandma Hensley gave me the good news about Crazy Bob, a raving lunatic who chain-sawed his way through electronic equipment on late-night TV ads. "You know," she told me in her sweet but matter-of-fact way, "when little Robbie was in my class he was always taking things from the other pupils, and then he would turn right around and try

91

to sell the stolen goods. Just imagine! It troubled me so. I'm awfully glad he's making an honest living now.")

There was some excited murmuring in the audience and then some scattered applause that gradually became loud and enthusiastic. "Crazy Bob, what a dude!" Danny yelled, and people really busted loose with laughter after that.

"And now here's Alex Mason," I said, encouraged by the audience's surging energy, "to tell you more about the Radical Wave."

Alex looked at me uncertainly. He wasn't wild about the idea of speaking in public, even to a group as small as this one. I gave him a reassuring smile as I sat down in a chair next to the podium, and Robin gave him an encouraging push. He walked to the podium and was greeted by loud applause.

"Ladies and gentlemen," he began nervously, "dudes and dudettes, I just want to echo what my good buddy T.J. said. We, the underprivileged of Westport High, have been ignored by our student leaders long enough. If they think they own this high school, they're dreamin' big time! It belongs to all of us! Student government is supposed to be a democracy, and we're going to see that it starts running like one. Power to the people!" Alex thrust his arms into the air in a victory sign.

Our embryonic club went wild, and Alex looked pretty surprised about the response he was getting. I was surprised, too. Behind those cool blue shades, the guy had been hiding some real charisma. "And now we need some hard-core input from you," Alex continued as the crowd quieted down. "We want to know what kind of club *you* want the Wave to be."

Vivian Chandler's hand shot up, and Alex gave her the floor. "What about the election of club officers?" she asked.

Alex shrugged and looked at me. "Well," I said, standing, "we, um, we haven't had our club officially chartered yet, so we were sort of waiting, and—"

"You want democracy, right?" Vivian challenged me as she also stood up. "So why not start right here, right now?"

"Righteous!" a surfer yelled. There was a lot of cheering for Vivian's idea, which had caught me completely off guard. I'd sort of figured that I'd appoint the first slate of officers. "Okay," I said, tossing the ball back into her court, "why don't you come on up here and conduct the elections yourself."

There were cheers and wolf whistles for

Vivian as she strutted onto the stage. "Okay, boys and girls," she said, leaning casually against the podium as if she did this sort of thing all the time, "we'll start with nominations for president."

Alex and I were both nominated, and then Sandbar Sam threw his support behind "bodacious Vivian Chandler." His action was greeted by wild cheering from the surfing delegation, but Vivian grinned at me and declined the nomination, explaining that she was more interested in becoming secretary-treasurer. (I had wondered what she was up to!) She was promptly nominated for that office by three different surfers. I then nominated an old friend, Eric Schaefer, for the job, because I'd promised it to him. He would be ticked off at me when he lost, but what could I do? Democracy was like that.

Just as Vivian started to call on the nominees to make their short speeches, the door to the classroom burst open and a small mob of unfriendly faces poured in.

"Party's over, Durant," David Whitworth said in a snide, supremely confident voice. He was accompanied by about ten leadership students and two campus security guards. Talk about overkill! (At least Janet wasn't with him.) "Go ahead, Sharilyn," David said to Sharilyn Reed, the commissioner of activities.

"According to student body bylaws," Sharilyn said nervously, as if club-smashing was not her idea of fun, "Article Thirty, Section C, Subsection A, you cannot meet on campus as a club until such time as your club charter has been formally accepted by the Student Leadership Council." Sharilyn then retreated behind her fearless leader, who folded his arms and invited a rebuttal.

We were all temporarily stunned into silence.

The shock wore off quickly, though, as students began to boo their student body president loudly, stomping their feet in protest.

"You're spun, dude!" Dizzy Danny said, looking in the general direction of David Whitworth. (Danny had trouble focusing on solid objects.) Other students made more graphic remarks.

"This is a conspiracy!" Eric Schaefer charged. (Eric wrote a conspiracy column for the school newspaper.)

Sandbar Sam began a chant—"Bo-gus! Bo-gus! Bo-gus!"—which just about everyone in the club was soon roaring at David Whitworth. The expression on David's face made it obvious that he hadn't expected such a rude challenge to his authority.

"They're going to riot!" Mike Geier wailed, his eyes wide with panic. "Call Dean Phelps!" he yelled at the security guards. They nodded and began to pull out their walkie-talkies.

"That won't be necessary!" I yelled at the security guards as I raised my hands in a gesture to calm the audience. I was suddenly tortured by visions of a gasping Radical Wave being strangled in its crib by a manic dean. "Quiet . . . please! Quiet! SHUT UP ALREADY!"

When everyone had finally settled down, I said to David, "Look, we don't want to give you an excuse to shut us down before we even get started. We know that's exactly what you'd like to do. So instead we're going to file out of here peacefully and walk on over to Sky Park across the street to finish the meeting. After all, you can't take away our right to assemble peacefully on public property."

We stood up together and began to march out of the room. Spider got to the door first, and when he did he turned to David and said, *"Hola, señor presidente. ¿Como está?"*

"Estoy bien, gracias. ¿Y usted?" David replied, obviously proud of his bilingual skills.

"Not so good," Spider said, pulling his hair away from his eyes. "You see, my family traveled thousands of miles at great risk to come to this country because they thought it was *free*, you know what I'm saying? And now I have to tell them that you can't even hold a meeting at the lousy high school without getting busted." Spider clicked the heels of his beach sandals together and gave a sharp salute. *"Se va a armar las de Dios es Cristo, general Wheet-worth. ¡Hasta la vista, pendejo!"*

Spider marched out the door, leaving a bewildered student body president in his wake. "What'd he say?!" David demanded.

Robin Frye smiled. "He says that all hell is going to break loose. *And* he thinks you're an idiot." The club members laughed and cheered as they filed out the door.

"But I *have* to enforce the rules," David sputtered. "Without rules, there would be chaos—"

Sandbar Sam began to sing "We Shall Overcome" in a terrific bass, and soon everyone joined in, except for an increasingly

97

dispirited crowd of red-faced leadership council members.

We crossed 17th Street and resettled on the grass in the park. It was really just a huge lawn that some developer had traded for the right to build some ugly pink condos near the beach, but hey, open space was open space. People were pretty riled up at first, and there was even some talk of sabotaging a leadership council meeting "just to see how they'd like it." Backed up by Alex and Vivian, I asked for patience and reminded them of the "Don't Fight It—Ride It" philosophy that had served Big Wave Dave so well.

"Hey, how come the big guy isn't here today?" Dizzy Danny wanted to know.

"I heard the Davester's out shreddin' some bitchin' sets down at the creek," another surfer explained.

Alex and I just smiled at each other.

Things went pretty smoothly after that. We made our speeches, cast our votes, and gathered suggestions for club projects and activities in the coming year. When all was said and done, I was president, Alex was vice-president, and Vivian was secretary-treasurer. As a club we decided that, in addition to taking on the senior center project, we would:

1. Recruit more club members.
2. Plant more trees in Westport Beach as a way of fighting air pollution.
3. Help clean up graffiti at school and at the beach.
4. Start a political accountability campaign aimed at the Student Leadership Council.
5. Recruit even more club members.

When the meeting ended, I kicked back on the grass with Vivian and thanked her for taking charge of elections. She smiled slyly and said, "Someone has to keep you honest, Durant."

I couldn't help noticing how beautiful her brown eyes were in the late afternoon sunlight. "Alex sure is hanging around with Robin Frye a lot lately," I said, feeling a little sorry for Vivian.

"Isn't that great?!" Vivian said enthusiastically. "Who would've *ever* put those two strangers together? I love it when stuff like that happens."

"But I thought you'd be, you know, *hurt*, or disappointed, or something. You told me a few weeks ago that Alex got you all hot and bothered—"

I was cut off by Vivian's laughter. She ripped up a handful of grass and chucked it at me. "I said that about his glasses, you dork!"

"Who are you calling a dork?" I said as I beaned her with an even larger handful of grass. She grabbed my throwing arm, I grabbed hers, and pretty soon we were laughing and wrestling and rolling on the grass, just like we used to do as little kids. But it didn't *feel* the same now as it had then, not by a long shot. I was enjoying myself in an entirely different way, and I could tell by the gleam in her eyes that she was, too.

"Sex alert!" Eric Schaefer yelled. He was always yelling lame stuff like that. Poor Eric wore glasses that were about an inch thick, and he had a big old orange mole on his chin that you could see from about a mile away. Girls scared the hell out of him, mainly because he'd never seen one up close. But his sex alert didn't go unnoticed. The crowd started razzing Vivian and me, and so we sat back up, brushed ourselves off, and told Eric that he was dead meat. He nervously consulted his calculator watch and then made a rapid exit, explaining that he had to go home and get to work on his column about today's big political scandal.

Scandal? I looked frantically across the street at the high school to see if Janet had been watching Vivian and me roll around in the grass. But of course, Janet was nowhere in sight. The campus was virtually deserted. Besides, so what if Janet *had* seen me with Vivian? This was no scandal. Vivian was a good friend. Vivian was . . . watching me very intently, I realized as I turned back to look at her. So intently, in fact, that I soon began to squirm like a bug under a magnifying glass.

"So," Vivian said, "old Janet didn't show up to attend the party *or* to crash it. Playing her cards kind of close to her pretty little chest these days, isn't she?"

Not so *little*, babe. "You know," I said, eager for a chance to defend Janet, "I think I figured out why she broke up with me. It was *her mother's* idea—"

Vivian surprised me by laughing.

"That by you is funny?" I asked.

"No," she said, shaking her head, "*you* are. You paint such a pretty picture of Little Miss Brooks, it's no wonder you're so crazy about her. Mother my *ass*! My mother tried for years to force me into ballet slippers. Do these look like ballet slippers to you?" she asked, laying her booted feet on my lap.

I angrily pushed the boots aside. "What? Are you trying to tell me that you didn't let your mother influence you at all? No wonder she packed up and moved to Michigan!"

Vivian looked so hurt that I was instantly sorry for opening my big mouth. I began apologizing all over the place, but Vivian just shook her head and said, "Pump your brakes, T.J. I probably deserved it. I've got no business taking such an interest in your screwed-up love life." She paused, gave me another long, probing look, and then said, "I just never pegged you as the social-climber type. I thought you made a pretty terrific outsider, you know?"

I thought that over for a moment. It was more or less the same thing Alex had said the night Janet dumped me. But it was so *exciting* on the inside and so *lonely* on the outside. . . .

"Just some food for thought, sailor," Vivian told me. She checked her watch, stood up, and brushed some more grass off her clothes. "I've gotta get home to protect Marcie from my overly affectionate father. Poor thing nearly gets crushed to death every time he hugs her." When I stood up, Vivian came over to me, slung one arm around my neck, kissed me on the cheek, and whispered, "This club is going to be *great.*"

She said her good-byes to everyone else and then crossed the street to catch a bus. I watched her departure with mixed feelings. Just when you thought you had Vivian pinned down as tough and insensitive, she kissed you on the cheek, whispered something nice into your ear, and left you feeling like—well, like you wanted *more.*

Vivian wasn't Janet, though. If only *Janet* had been at the meeting, if only *she* could've seen me stand up to David Whitworth. (He'd really blown it, actually, and not just because he'd been outclassed by Spider Martinez. David's power-tripping had succeeded in uniting the Wave at its first meeting in a way that no amount of pizza and speeches ever could have.) Well, Janet was sure to hear about what happened, one way or another. And on Friday, I'd get to make my pitch to the leadership council. I'd show her then.

Alex ran over to me while I was still lost in thought and asked if I'd ride with him to work. Robin had gone back to the band room to practice her clarinet. "Is there anything Robin *can't* do?" I asked as we ran across 17th Street to get our bikes.

"Yeah, she can't believe she's finally got a guy interested in her," Alex said, laughing.

As we rode out of the student lot and down to Pacific Coast Highway, Alex talked on and on about Robin and how well they got along together. "And to think I owe it all to you and your screwed-up love life, T.J. I never would've gone to that loser party if it hadn't been for you," he said.

"Only too happy to help," I replied.

We came to a stop at the intersection where 17th Street met the highway and watched the tan, the loony, and the beautiful zoom by. I looked out at the hazy blue Pacific horizon and wondered what exotic women and strange adventures might lie just beyond the curve of the Earth. Alex was telling me that Robin had invited him to dinner and a movie on Friday night. They were going to see a foreign film about Japanese fishermen—the sharks they subdued and the women they loved. "We were wondering if you'd like to come along," he said. "Double date."

"Gosh, yes," I said, "but only if Godzilla's

in it. Get *real*, Alex. Who'm I gonna ask to come with me—Janet?"

"How about Vivian? You two seemed to be getting pretty, um, close this afternoon." He smiled at me, but I didn't smile back. "Look," he said, "we're just talking a night at the movies. It's not like you'll have to sign a marriage contract or anything." The light changed, and we crossed the highway.

"I don't think so," I said, shaking my head as we rode toward 12th Street, where the Bistro was located. "Vivian can be a real pain at times, and besides, what if Janet found out?"

Alex held his wrists together above his head and said, "What, are you Janet's little love slave now? Come on, we're just talking about *one night* here. You need to do something besides lust after Janet twenty-four hours a day. It's getting boring, bud."

I was getting boring? Really? *Boring?* "Okay, I'll call Vivian and ask her. But I'm only doing it because it was your idea. And she just might say no, wise man."

We arrived at the Bistro, which was a sort of '40s retro diner with Hawaiian ambience. Over the main entrance was a sign depicting a hula girl on a skateboard. At night she did a skateboard-hula dance in neon. Inside the restaurant there was a grove of plastic palm trees that had pumpkins and apples hanging from their fronds and a giant aquarium filled with multicolored plastic fish and wind-up lobsters. (A wind-up lobster derby was held once a month.) Bogus all the way, for sure, except for the fantastic hamburgers.

Alex smiled as he locked up his bike and said, "From what I saw this afternoon, I have a feeling Vivian'll say yes."

Before I could explain to him about our innocent wrestling match, he disappeared behind the door marked EMPLOYEES ONLY. He probably wouldn't have believed me anyway.

That night as I microwaved frozen pizzas for my sister Gretchen and myself, I decided not to call Vivian. It'd be unfair to give her the wrong idea. But then I asked Gretchen for her opinion as we ate dessert, and she said, "It's just a date, T.J. Can I put marshmallows in my ice cream, please?"

I sprinkled some miniature marshmallows on Gretchen's ice cream, tossed a few into Chester's mouth, and then decided that maybe I should call Vivian after all.

I did my math, English, and science homework. I cleaned my room, loaded the dishwasher, took Chester for a walk, and did some laundry. I watched a sitcom on TV at nine o'clock but was too distracted to laugh very much. I was running out of time.

The phone rang, and Gretchen ran from her room to get it. She was supposed to be in bed by now. "T.J.!—It's—for—you!" she yelled. She loved to announce phone calls that way, even when there was only one other person in the house.

"It's Janet," she whispered shrilly as I took the phone.

"Go to bed," I whispered back. "Mom and Dad'll be home any second, and if you're still up you're gonna get it!"

Gretchen squealed and ran back to her room.

"Hi, Janet," I said, jazzed that she'd called. "What's up?"

"Bad news, I'm afraid. David's doing everything he can to keep your club from being chartered on Friday. He's trying to convince every member of the council that *your* service club would be one service club too many. He's also telling everyone that your club almost rioted in the drama classroom today. Is that true?"

I had to laugh. The *slime*. "It's pure B.S., and I've got plenty of witnesses who'll back me up. You want me to bring them all to the meeting on Friday?"

"No! No. Look, I want to support you in this, T.J. It's the least I can do for you, after all the help you've given me. But you can't ignore the fact that David *is* student body president, which means he pulls a lot of weight on the council."

"Why would you leave me for a jerk like him?" I asked, mad enough now not to care about her feelings.

"Look, I didn't call you because I wanted to get personal. I just wanted to warn you about Friday, so you could be prepared, okay?"

"What would you suggest I do?"

"Have you thought about changing the name of the club?"

"Not a chance. No way. Forget it."

"Well, then all I can say is you'd better make sure your presentation is outstanding. And don't come on too strong. You know how you make people nervous."

What was wrong with making people nervous? People needed to be nervous every now and then!

I had to calm down before I said something stupid. I took a few deep breaths and stabbed a pen into the cork message board by the phone. I reassured myself that I had Janet's vote and that she'd cared enough to call me. She didn't *have* to call me, but she had. "Well, thanks a lot," I said sincerely. "I appreciate the advice. By the way, would you like to go out to the movies with me on Friday night?" What the hell. I had nothing to lose by asking.

There was a long pause, so long that I began to think that she might've hung up on me. "I swear, you are so *out* of it sometimes," Janet finally said. "You know I'm with David now. I'm calling as your *friend*. In fact, it took me a long time to get up the nerve to call you at all. If he were to find out—"

"He won't," I quickly assured her. "I'll swear to my grave that this conversation never occurred. Later."

"T.J., don't—"

I hung up. Out of it? *I* was out of it? *I* wasn't the one going out with someone who needed ten bodyguards to protect himself from the students he supposedly represented.

My parents came home soon after I hung up on Janet, and I was still so mad that I barely said hello to them before I dialed Vivian's number. "Isn't it a little late to be making phone calls?" my mom asked me.

"Isn't it a little late to be parenting?" I shot back. I'd taken care of Gretchen for two nights in a row, and it was getting to me. My mother gave me a hurt look and then left me alone. I'd have to apologize for that crack before I went to bed or I'd never hear the end of it.

"Hi, Viv," I said when she answered the phone. "T.J. here. You wanna go out on a double date with Alex and Robin on Friday night? You know, dinner and a flick?"

There was a long pause. Girls seemed to be specializing in long pauses tonight. "I'd love to," she finally said. She sounded pretty stoked about the idea, which gave my spirits a boost. "If I'd known you'd react this way, T.J., I'd've started insulting your judgment a lot sooner. What are we going to see?"

"I don't know. Some Japanese art film that doesn't star Godzilla."

"You're twisted. What should I wear?"

Why did girls always ask questions like that? "Nothing at all. It's a nude theater, and there's going to be an orgy during intermission."

"I'll bring some whipped cream, then," she

said, laughing. A long silence followed, and finally Vivian said, "Well, good night, T.J., and thanks!"

"Well, good night, Viv, and same to you!"

When I hung up, I went to my parents' room right away, kissed my mom on the cheek, and apologized.

She nodded approvingly and took my hand. "You know, T.J., your father and I work awfully hard to give you kids everything you need."

Violins began to play in my head. Soon she'd tell me about how she'd had to drive her convertible several blocks to Stanford every day in the pouring sun, just to get through college. "I know, Mom," I said mechanically.

I could've challenged her statement. I had before, but I was too tired to really get into an argument about moral philosophy, greed, and twisted values. Besides, she might get mad at me and cut off my allowance.

"You shouldn't talk to your mother that way, young man," my dad said. He was removing his vest. I was pretty sure he'd been born in a three-piece suit.

"I know, Dad," I said mechanically. (I loved my parents and all, but they could be *such* a hassle sometimes.)

Mom smiled at me and said, "Grandma told me all about your new club, by the way. I think it's a wonderful idea."

"You're starting a club?" my father said. He sounded surprised and sort of intrigued. I eagerly told him all about the Radical Wave, and when I was done he said he liked everything about the club except its name. "It sounds rather like a brand of insecticide."

I explained about the name, though, and then Dad shook my hand and said, "Good work, Thomas."

Another major compliment from my dad. I'd be amped for weeks!

Seven As it turned out, my euphoria only lasted until Friday morning, when I sat down to pitch the Radical Wave to a poker-faced Student Leadership Council. I calmed my nerves by imagining that all twenty members had just finished competing in a violent nude mud-wrestling contest.

Sharilyn Reed formally introduced me to the council, although I'd already met and gotten friendly with most of these students over the summer. They didn't look any too friendly now, though. Sharilyn then invited me to present my club proposal. I decided to focus on Janet as I spoke, even though she avoided making eye contact with me throughout most of my presentation. My proposal, which was basically just a review of club goals and the means for reaching them, was aided by incredibly detailed color computer graphics created by Robin and Alex on Robin's home computer. The best pair of graphics, which were actually Vivian's idea, portrayed a treeless, smog-choked, graffiti-infested neighborhood populated with apathetic high school students and desperately lonely senior citizens; and then the same neighborhood transformed into a cleaner, healthier environment through the efforts of the Radical Wave. What the graphics lacked in subtlety they more than made up for in visual impact. The entire council seemed to sit up and take notice.

When I finished my presentation, Sharilyn asked if there were any questions, and Mike Geier nodded eagerly. "Isn't your club redundant? Doesn't it just create an overabundance of service clubs on this campus? Isn't it, in fact, superfluous and excessive?" he asked, reading from a three-by-five card and mispronouncing "superfluous."

"Did you sleep with a thesaurus under your pillow last night, or what?" I asked him, and there were some giggles and titters from the council members. Janet, though, shook her head slightly and gave me a disapproving look.

David Whitworth glared at Janet for this bit of coaching, and then he turned to me and said, "I think the point our commissioner of education is trying to make here is that while many of your ideas may be good ones, we wonder why you couldn't simply implement them as a member of one of our long-established service clubs."

"That's my point *exactly*," Mike said, beaming at his boss.

"And it's a *good* point, too," I said with mock enthusiasm. I was ready for this question. "Now, if you'll just tell me, guys, which of our distinguished service clubs will *guarantee* me, and people like me, membership, I'll be happy to join right up!"

My challenge stimulated quite a bit of discussion, which didn't die down until David banged his gavel a few times. "Come on, T.J.," said Rich Myers, senior class president, "nobody's *guaranteed* membership in the service clubs. You know that as well as we do. But that doesn't mean—"

"It means everything," I said, cutting him off. "It all comes down to membership. Look, I'm not slamming the other service clubs here. They do a great job. I just want to start a nonexclusive service club, a service club whose only membership requirement is *the desire to serve*."

That stirred up even more discussion and more gavel-banging. "What sort of requirements do you think the other service clubs impose?" Daysi Ortega, student body vice-president asked me with a smile. She was a cool kitty with class to spare. I'd voted for her without hesitation last year and had encouraged Janet to take notes on Daysi's friendly, intelligent, no-B.S. style.

"Oh, you know," I said, smiling back, "dress codes, credit checks, blood tests, family background investigations by the FBI. That sort of thing." The crowd responded with a loud mixture of laughter and angry protests. (Janet, however, remained conspicuously silent.)

David began to bang his gavel again, but Mr. Ito, who'd been standing unobtrusively in the corner of the room, stepped forward and shook his tanned, gray-haired head. "Let's act like leaders here, people," he instructed the council calmly, and the room instantly got quiet.

Tad Nguyen, junior class rep, turned to me and said, "There are some council members who feel that your club will be radical in a negative way. You know, like destructive and out of control. How would you respond to this charge?"

This *charge*? "Unless you consider our red T-shirts and rainbow-tinted sunglasses to represent an act of violence," I said gravely, "I believe the hallways of Westport High will

116

continue to be safe for women and small children." Some council members smiled.

There was a long pause, and then Mike Yee, the temporary representative for the freshman class, asked, "Just how do you make this triple-thick pizza, anyway?"

His question provoked a lot of laughter from the council members, and even Mr. Ito joined in. "It's simple, really," I said. "You pile three layers of cheese, sauce, and toppings on, instead of just one or two. It requires a very sturdy crust, of course."

There were a few more easy-to-field inquiries and comments about the club, and then everyone, except Janet, turned to the student body president for his response. (By this point Janet had her head bowed and her hands folded, as if she were praying for deliverance.)

David cleared his throat dramatically and then asked me in an openly hostile voice, "How'd you come up with the idea for this so-called Radical Wave of yours?"

All the members of the council turned to look at me. Obviously, they put a lot of weight on the questions their president asked.

I reminded them of the campaign promises Janet had made (with my encouragement)—

promises to increase student involvement in campus and community service. I admitted that my initial concern for the senior center was largely inspired by a desire to help my own grandparents, but then I told them how Spider Martinez and Sandbar Sam Utu had helped me to see the bigger picture. I also mentioned the surfer who'd cruised by me at the marina, and I described how his casual greeting had helped me come up with the name for the club.

"I'm sure we're all very moved by your devotion to senior citizens," David said with acid sarcasm, "but we can hardly be expected to charter a club just so you can take a little ego trip to impress your granny. Especially," he said, shaking the gavel at me, "when we know from past experience just how destructive your little ego trips can be!"

My granny?! He was getting personal— even Janet seemed appalled by his remarks. "Hey, *Mister* President," I said, trying hard to control my growing outrage, "if you want to talk about ego trips, why don't we discuss the one you took to the drama department on Wednesday afternoon?"

"You're skating on thin ice here, David,"

Daysi interjected over a rising tide of agitated discussion.

"No! No, I'm not. You don't seem to get it, people. This guy," David said, waving the gavel at me again, "is starting this club for no other reason than his own personal gain. He's doing it to draw attention to himself, not to help others. He just wants to be popular, especially in the eyes of a certain girl, and that is *no* reason to start a club!"

I was so shocked to hear him publicly allude to Janet that I almost laughed out loud. He'd really stepped in it now.

Janet gave him a stunned, betrayed look, while most of the other council members just looked plain stunned. "You just fell *through* the ice," Daysi said to David as she shook her head in disgust. She turned to look directly at Janet and added, "I don't think our personal feelings and problems should have *any* influence on council decisions. That would be just plain wrong."

Janet blushed cherry red and began to stare at the tabletop.

David glared at his V.P. "So you think we—or rather, *I*—should disqualify myself from voting, is that it?" he challenged Daysi.

"It makes no difference to me *what* you decide to do," Daysi countered. "Your vote is only one among many here, and I for one think that T.J., with *your* help, has made a very powerful case for the need to open up our service club roster to some, shall we say, *underrepresented* minority groups."

This blistering exchange was followed by a long, uncomfortable silence, which was broken only when Sharilyn Reed asked me, with obvious reluctance: "Do you have any final remarks to make before we take a vote?"

I looked uncertainly at Daysi, and she gave me an encouraging nod. I stood up and said, "Our distinguished president is at least half-right about my motives. But we all have some selfish motives for serving others, when you get right down to it. You can ask yourselves, for example, why you like serving on this council. It's important to help your school, sure, but it's not doing you any harm, either—popularitywise, powerwise, and otherwise.

"The fact is, the Radical Wave belongs at Westport High. It belongs here because of what it stands for, not because of what *I* may personally get out of it. If you give it a chance, I know the Radical Wave will be around to serve this school long after I've graduated.

And that's the whole point behind chartering a club, right?" I was making this up as I went along, but I thought it ended up sounding pretty good.

Most of the council members applauded, and then I was asked to wait outside during the vote.

As soon as I was out the door, my heart started to race and my stomach knotted up again. Thank God for Daysi Ortega! If she hadn't stood up to David, I might not have mustered the nerve to make that final speech. And what was Janet's problem, anyway? She hadn't said a word! Not one word of support for my constructive idea, an idea that she'd helped to inspire. What a hypocrite she was!

Of course, it wasn't her fault. Not really. David was obviously keeping her on a leash.

I stood as close to the door as I dared, listening as the indecipherable murmur of voices rose and fell like a gusting wind. As the bell to end fifth period rang, David burst out of the office and pinned me against the wall before I had a chance to react. "You may have won *this* time, little man, but you'll live to regret it," he said bitterly, letting me go and then storming off toward the quad.

It took me a few seconds to recover. "Well,

thank *you*, Mr. President!" I shouted. "We look forward to your good-natured support!"

Janet ran out of the office next, yelling, "David, wait up!"

I impulsively grabbed her by the arm and said, "Don't run after him, Janet. He's a loser!"

She wrenched her arm away from me and said miserably, "Oh, T.J., you've messed up everything."

"But I thought you'd be happy for me," I said. She couldn't possibly feel sorry for David, could she? Wasn't it clear by now that he was a full-on jerk?

"Oh, of course I am! You've divided up the council, driven away David, and utterly humiliated me, all in less than an hour!"

"But what choice did I have—David never even gave the club a chance. You told me so yourself!"

She pressed her fingertips against her temples and said, "I've got a terrible headache, and it's got T.J. Durant written all over it. Your club deserved to be chartered, it *was* chartered, and now you can go out tonight with Vivian Chandler and celebrate, okay? Now *please* get out of my way!"

Janet already knew about my date with

Vivian? "Hey," I said desperately, "just say the word, and I'll call it off. I mean it."

For a moment Janet seemed surprised and even a little touched by my offer, but then her blue eyes hardened and she said, "I couldn't care less who you go out with. You're trouble. No matter what happens between David and me, I'm not coming back to you." Her eyes began to well up with tears, and this apparently involuntary display of grief seemed to enrage her all the more. *"Get out of my life!"* she shrieked as she ran off in search of her wounded hero.

"Gladly!" I yelled after her. But I didn't sound too convincing, even to myself.

I went to sit out the lunch period under the visitors' bleachers, amid other discarded trash. I was too sick to eat anything anyway. Janet hated me. Life sucked massively. Westport High was run by a clique of stuck-up rich kids who only dated other stuck-up rich kids. My thing with Janet had been fluke, a summer mirage. Alex had been right all along.

I was thinking about quitting high school to join the Coast Guard when Alex found me. I was sort of hoping he'd show up.

"So the Wave is official," he said as he sat

down next to me. He'd brought along the grocery bag he loaded with snacks and kept in his locker. He pulled out a package of chocolate cupcakes and tossed it into my lap. "Let's celebrate," he said in a distinctively nonfestive voice.

I opened the package and started munching. I discovered that I was hungry after all. "Janet hates me," I said. I told him all about the meeting and what'd happened afterward.

Alex ripped the wrapping off a lemon pie and said, "Yeah, I've already heard about some of it. I saw Janet in the quad, probably just a few minutes after she left you. She was crying all over the place and saying that you'd ruined her life. David is apparently thinking about breaking up with her, after only two weeks."

What? "But that's great!" I said.

Alex swallowed a mouthful of lemon pie and said, "Get over yourself, T.J. He's just bluffing, and you know it. Janets don't grow on trees, not even in *his* neighborhood. No, he was upset that she voted to charter the Wave, and he wanted to punish her for her disloyalty. When he thinks she's learned her lesson, he'll forgive her. Just so long as she promises never to take your side again."

"She wouldn't promise that," I said uncertainly as I started in on my second cupcake. "You don't know Janet the way I do."

Alex shook his head. "Sometimes I wonder if I know *you* anymore, bud. You're obsessed with Janet Brooks, and not in a good way. You need to do some heavy-duty introspecting here. Is it really Janet you love or is it just the lifestyle of the high school rich and famous that you lust after?"

I glared at him, but he eventually stared me down. The worst thing about his question was that I really didn't know the answer to it. Could he be right?

After a long, uncomfortable silence, Alex tossed me a package of Twinkies and smiled reassuringly. "Don't sweat it too much, chumley. There's hope for you yet. You're going out with Vivian Chandler tonight, and she's as down-to-earth as they come."

I laughed with relief. *That* was something we could both agree on.

Eight My mom was standing at the bathroom door, looking sharp in her gold-colored real estate blazer. I wasn't sure what I wanted to do for a living when I got older, but I certainly wasn't going to try to sell houses to people. Mom spent a ton of time working and complained a lot about the rude types who came to look at open houses when they had no intention of buying. They just wanted decorating ideas or were bored and wanted to kill an afternoon, Mom said. I knew she didn't make much money from her job because I heard her fight with my father about it every now and then, especially when the market was "soft," like now. Dad wanted Mom to go back to school and finish her Ph.D. in art history, but Mom said that Ph.D.'s were for people who were afraid of spending time outside of libraries.

"Who're you going out with, honey?" she asked me. She seemed excited that I was going out, like it was my first date or something.

"Vivian Chandler," I said as I recombed my hair for the sixth time.

"Little Vivian?" she asked.

"She's not so little anymore, Mom."

She gave me one of those sad, oh-where-do-the-years-go looks and said, "No, of course not. Well, it's nice to see you dating again."

"It's only been two weeks!"

"Well, of course it has, T.J.," she said, patting my shoulder gently.

Mothers!

I took off before she could interrogate me further. I was supposed to meet Vivian, Alex, and Robin at the Spanish Main restaurant for dinner at six-thirty, and I was planning to drop by Janet's place on the way. I *had* to know where I stood with her before I saw Vivian.

I took a circuitous route to the Brooks place so that I could scope it out without being spotted. Ms. Brooks's lavender Jag was parked in the driveway, and David Whitworth's Beemer was out on the street. After doing the betrayed lover routine at lunch, he was already back at Janet's house for dinner! I kicked two of David's tires to set off his car alarm and raced off to the restaurant.

Vivian was wearing a red scoop-neck sweater and white velour leggings. She'd styled her hair so that it crested up from the part, cascaded down the right side of her face, and swept her shoulder in a thoroughly seductive wave. She looked so pretty that I had to force myself not to stare at her.

Alex had had his hair *cut* for the occasion, and he was wearing a shirt with an honest-to-God collar—he looked downright upright. Robin, with her hair unpinned and a 1,000-watt smile periodically lighting up her usually dour countenance, was doing a terrific impersonation of an attractive, laid-back southern California blond who was stepping out on the town for a good time.

The Spanish Main faced the waterfront and was furnished to look like the interior of an old Spanish galleon. Masts, booms, brass lanterns, ropes, cargo-hold covers, and bits of canvas sail hung down from the ceiling, and the partitions between the booths resembled old sea chests. Wall murals depicted pirate battles, lost treasure, violent storms, and brave conquistadors, and each tabletop featured a resin-covered map of the world circa 1600. Vivian, Alex, and I thought it was all pretty cool, but Robin called it a "reckess, commercial distortion of history." I had to smile. That was almost *exactly* what my father had said about the place.

The teriyaki steak and shrimp tasted great, and the conversation never died—or even came close. We toasted the chartering of the Wave about a million times, Vivian told sailing stories, Robin discussed politics and the decline of American civilization, and Alex touted the superiority of trailers over traditional homes. "They're so much easier to clean," he told us. Robin and Alex also kept at it with the sonnets all through dinner:

Alex: " 'Let me not to the marriage of true minds admit impediments.' "

Robin: " 'Love is not love which alters when it alteration finds.' "

And so on. It got sort of annoying after a while, but I wasn't going to complain. I'd never seen Alex fall so hard for a girl. Vivian and I shed our shoes and started communicating with our feet shortly after the appetizers were served. This continued throughout dinner, though Vivian never let my feet move above her ankles.

After dinner we walked over to the Crestline Theater at Main and Electric. The Crestline had seen its glory days when James Dean was still alive, and now smelled of dust, ancient popcorn, and moldy velvet. It played movies that were too out of it for the mall scene—foreign films and arty stuff that only critics and uptight academics like Robin and my dad wanted to see. The movie Robin had recommended was sold out! She was bummed, but the rest of us were pretty much relieved. We took a bus down the Pacific Coast Highway to the Marina Mall Cinemas and decided to watch *Vampire Ninjas Must Die!* because it started in just ten minutes.

Unlike the Crestline, the Marina Mall Cinemas were first-rate, with fresh red carpeting, a video-game room, two snack bars, oversized chandeliers, mirrors on most of the walls, huge cardboard displays for soon-to-be-released films, and bathrooms so clean you'd let your grandmother use them.

Apparently, Robin was not impressed by the decor.

"Aren't *ninjas* Japanese?" Vivian asked, trying to cheer Robin up a little.

She shook her head and grumbled about "gratuitous violence" and "teen exploitation." She did lighten up a little, though, when we bought a jumbo bucket of popcorn, two boxes of frozen bonbons, and four boxes of assorted candy.

We scarfed heavily as we watched the vampire *ninjas* almost wipe out a small New England town. The adults were disappearing one by one, and no one in the clueless village could figure out why. Then a group of students did some investigating and found out that the new high school had been built over an old graveyard. (The school board had obviously never been to see a horror movie.) The graveyard contained the remains of some *ninjas* who'd immigrated to America in the late 19th century. The *ninjas* had been ambushed and killed by a group of townspeople who, for reasons never explained, thought the *ninjas* had come from Japan to buy up all their farms and leave them jobless.

The students told their principal and the town leaders what was going down, but of course none of the adults would listen. Pretty soon most of these ignorant postadolescents were vampire *ninjas* themselves, and they were going after the students. The students started watching martial-arts videos and learned the subtle art of stake-driving. In practically no time at all, they were experts at hand-to-hand combat and the killing of vampires. The final battle was a gory mess, but the students won in the end because all the *ninja* vampires were trapped on the school athletic field when the sun rose and they burst into flames.

"It was bloody, but was it art?" Alex asked as the credits rolled.

"Oscar Wilde said all art is quite useless. That was a totally useless movie, so it must be totally great art," I reasoned.

"I think I ate too much popcorn," Vivian said, rubbing her stomach.

"So nobody minds if I polish off the red licorice?" Alex asked. Nobody did.

Robin surprised us by saying that she liked the movie. "I expected gory, mass-market trash," she said, "and I was not disappointed. But the thoughtful commentary on racial attitudes and their relationship to international economic competition was quite provocative."

It was clear, at least to me, that Robin had eaten too many bonbons.

"I wonder if there'll be a sequel," Alex said.

"For sure there will be," Vivian replied. "The head *ninja* got away before the sun came up."

"He was fried!" Alex countered, and Robin agreed with him. I couldn't remember what'd happened to the head *ninja*, so I took Vivian's side.

We argued about the *ninja's* fate for a while in front of the theater, and then Robin said that she had to call it a night. "I have synchronized swimming lessons on Saturday morning," she explained. Alex left with her, and Vivian and I decided to walk around the marina to look at the boats in the moonlight.

There's no place more peaceful than a marina at night. The water's usually smooth as glass, the docks gently creak and groan as the boats tug at them, and the masts and rigging of the sailboats make a nice frame for the stars. And on a moonlit night, the marina is at its best, because the boats look like phantom ships on a silver sea.

Vivian and I sat down on a bench near the harbormaster's office, where we had a good view of the big sloops and schooners. They were tall and sleek, designed for some deep-water adventure. Vivian gazed at them with the same kind of soulful longing that I felt. "Remember that game we used to play as kids, where we'd imagine that we each had our very own island to run, anyway we wanted?" she asked.

I grinned and nodded as I remembered an island piled high with candy and treasure. No girls were allowed.

"What would your island be like now?" she wanted to know.

I thought it over for a few minutes. "I guess I'd pick an island in the North Pacific, one of those places where the trees are bent into fantastic shapes by the wind, and where the fog and rain cause dark green forests to spring up on the hillsides, and where wildflowers of all colors bloom. . . ."

I was getting a little carried away with the sound of my own words, but I was having too much fun to stop. "I'd build a house near a cliff edge, and watch the storms and the calms and the migration of whales. I'd write sea adventure stories under an assumed name and become famous but never reveal my true identity. . . . And then," I added, "a beautiful, determined woman would fall in love with me because of my stories, and she'd search the world until at last she found my island. We'd spend the rest of our lives there together, sharing our warm, gentle love as we enjoyed the harsh, spectacular beauty—"

Vivian interrupted my fantasy with a real, live kiss. It was a very *Vivian* sort of kiss—lively, forceful, and extremely stimulating.

"You've gotten better at this game," she said afterward.

"Thanks," I said breathlessly. "The prizes have gotten better, too. . . . And what about *your* island?"

Vivian traced her island on my chest with one finger and said, "Mine would be in the South Pacific—sunny, sultry, and just *lousy* with lush, fertile jungles and loud, exotic animals. I'd run a retreat there for the children of divorce." She sat up, and assumed a speaker's pose. "I'd hold seminars with titles like The Care and Feeding of Nervous Stepparents and Get Real!—Talk Fast!: Making the Most of Those Long-Distance Phone Calls. . . . Of course, I'd probably need an island the size of Australia to accommodate all my prospective clients."

We laughed together, and she laid her head against my shoulder. I wondered how she got her hair to smell so good. It was actually shimmering a little in the moonlight. "T.J.," she asked me, almost in a whisper, "where do things *really* stand with you and Janet?"

I stroked her hair and asked casually, "Who's Janet?"

Vivian gazed up at me with her big, beautiful, brown eyes and said, "Seriously. Are you still in love with her or what? I'm not the kind of girl who likes to kiss for practice."

"I don't think. . . . I mean, there's nothing. . . . That is to say, probably *not*."

Vivian laughed at me, and then we kissed again. I held onto it a little too long this time, and she finally had to push me away—gently. "Relax," she said with a caring smile. "You don't have to get it all at once. *I'll* still be around tomorrow."

"I sure hope so," I said, smiling back.

We walked all the way back to her house and kissed once more at her doorstep. I wasn't worrying anymore about who might be watching us.

Nine With the club chartered, the Radical Wave was ready to roll. Or so we'd hoped. But raffle ticket and T-shirt sales were pretty dismal at first. As usual, apathy seemed to be the favorite cause at Westport High. Students and Westport Beach residents had all kinds of lame excuses for not buying tickets or T-shirts: They'd already given to other worthy causes. They were saving money for college. Their dog needed braces. The index of leading economic indicators was down. Mercury was in Uranus on their star charts. . . . Students were less inclined to give dumb excuses to Sandbar Sam, so they often just ran for their lives when he approached.

Alex, Vivian, and I were forced to call an emergency summit meeting. We decided we needed to start running this fund-raiser like a political campaign, which meant pulling out all the stops. My first idea was to produce a flyer featuring a photograph of the regulars at the senior center (including Grandma and Grandpa Hensley and Spider's *abuelita*) over the caption "Help these ex-teenagers to get a life—give to the Ocean View Senior Recreation Center." The three of us also came up with various slogans for buttons, flyers, and posters: Buy a Tree and Save Your Mother; Wave if You Gave; Spend for Radical Change; Help Keep Grandparents Off the Streets; Smile if You're Radically Involved; and Show the World How Generous You Are and You Might Win a VCR!

It took a week, and nearly all the money we'd raised so far, to get the promotional materials together. Some members of our fledgling club were already threatening to quit, saying the whole idea had been a radical mistake. I managed to convince them, at least temporarily, that the causes we were supporting were easily worth the risks we were taking.

Inside, though, I was feeling anxious and a little sick. I began to worry that, after hyping this thing to the max, I'd done nothing but set myself up for a terrible fall. Marketing an attractive candidate like Janet Brooks was one thing, but trying to get students to give to a charitable cause and care about their environment was something else entirely.

Janet had been keeping a very low profile, at least around me. Our brief encounters were all sweetness and no substance—the conversational equivalent of diet soda. Vivian put a lot of patient effort into shoring up my spirits, and it wasn't too long before we were seeing each other almost every night. We worked on club stuff, sweated over our lit crit assignments together (we had the same English class), kicked back in front of the TV, swapped favorite novels, and even gave each other free osculation lessons. We also continued to double-date with Alex and Robin.

In the first few days of the new campaign, in spite of all our best efforts, it really did look like we'd bit the big one. Ticket and T-shirt sales increased only slightly. But then we persuaded the school paper, *The Rookery*, to run a story about our campaign, and soon the local city paper, the *Westport Beach Journal*, did the same.

The articles apparently got people to take a closer look at what we were trying to do, and requests for buttons (far and away the best gauge of enthusiasm for a cause like ours) finally began to trickle in. The trickle gradually became a stream, and then the stream turned into a torrent. We had to order more buttons. And T-shirts. And raffle tickets. As sales increased, more students began to ask about joining the club. Eventually, "veteran" Rad Wavers actually began to complain about the influx of "wannabes." Teachers and administrators started to commend us for being socially responsible. I knew we'd really made it, though, when our flyers began to disappear from school walls, only to be replaced with flyers from other clubs. In high school, sabotage is the sincerest form of flattery.

To make a long story short, we sold over 3,000 tickets in the next four weeks and almost 250 T-shirts. Up until the last week, Spider and Sam ran virtually neck and neck for the lead in ticket sales, but Sam edged Spider out by giving up two consecutive afternoons of surfing so that he'd have more time to pound on doors. "It's kind of extreme, what Sam did," Spider said good-naturedly. "*Se volvio loco*—he went crazy, I think. But if the dude wants to win that bad, I won't stand in his way." Sam, as top salesperson, won a VCR—right along with the four raffle-ticket winners.

The raffle rally took place at lunch on a Friday, in the home bleachers on the football field. There was a lot of heavy-duty excitement in the crowd, with people comparing raffle-ticket numbers and showing off their Radical Wave buttons and T-shirts. During the past month, our club had more than doubled in size, and the fact that hundreds of people were willing to come out and sit in the stands on that hot, smoggy October day (you didn't have to be at the rally to win, as detailed on the tickets) meant that we had a lot of outside supporters, too.

Sam was so stoked at the rally that he hugged Crazy Bob. (As the master of ceremonies, Bob proved he really *was* crazy when, in spite of the heat, he wore his lumberjack costume from his TV commercials and lugged around his famous "price-slashing" chainsaw.) Sam was practically in tears by the time he took hold of the microphone. He told the crowd that he was "freaking out with gratitude," and he made a special point of letting Spider know that he could "come on over and use the VCR anytime." Sam went on to say that everybody, "even grommets," could be successful if they just "took off behind the peak and stuck it in there." He concluded with the advice: "Don't ever be afraid to do some serious lip damage!" Most of us were unclear about what he meant, but the surfers in the crowd cheered like crazy.

Even before the rally, Tuesday, our club meeting day, had started to become a sort of unofficial Radical Wave dress-up day at Westport High. We encouraged participation through announcements in the daily home-room bulletin, and students in red shirts, turquoise canvas shorts, and rainbow-tinted sunglasses began to show up, alone and in groups, all over campus. The trend was caus-ing the leadership council to "stress out heav-ily," according to several reliable sources. A lot of radically attired students were not ac-tually involved in the club, but we appreciated the free advertising.

Dean Phelps told me on one particularly radical Tuesday that he believed we were vi-olating the school dress code in some way and that "strict enforcement would be forthcom-ing." He never followed through on his threat, though. He was too busy dealing with the real problems on campus, like substance abuse, bad plumbing, truancy, and raucous gum-chewing.

Alex had started a graffiti-eradication pro-gram at school and the beach. He and his band

of Graffiti Thrashers went to city hall and vol-
unteered to "help this town clean up its act."
The brass at city hall liked the idea and even
donated cleaning materials. Alex and his
Thrashers, working when they could on afternoons, evenings, and weekends, wiped out
everything from Locals Only slogans to strings
of profanities that'd made even hard-core
surfers choke in amazement.

One of Alex's best Thrashers was, of all
people, Robin Frye. She said she "found the
activity both stimulating and rewarding," not
to mention it gave her an excuse to toss her
killer schedule aside for a few hours and hang
out with Alex. The two of them tutored each
other. "She's teaching me to manage my time
better," Alex told me, "and I'm teaching her
how to *un*manage hers."

Vivian, along with Eric Schaefer, was co-
ordinating the tree-planting program with the
city. Eric was interested in the tree project
because he was really stressing about the
greenhouse effect. "Westport Beach will be
nothing but a rest area for fish in a few decades
if we don't stop the global warming trend,"
he'd tell his wide-eyed volunteers—and he had
the computer models to prove it.

My project for the club was to conduct a

series of informational interviews with members of the leadership council for the school TV news broadcast. David Whitworth refused to cooperate at first, until Eric Schaefer wrote a scathing editorial for the school newspaper entitled: "What Is Our President Trying to Hide—and Why?"

David then agreed to an interview, which turned out to be pretty much of a surprise for me in that he proved to be articulate and informed on most school issues. He even had some halfway-decent activities lined up for the next few months. He cracked some jokes, too—of the funny variety. I was actually starting to wonder if maybe I'd been wrong about the guy—at least in terms of his commitment to the school—but then he finished up our interview by saying, "Of course, the student body can accomplish great things only as a unit. We are the Westport High Sea Lions, roaring proud of our school. There is a certain club on this campus, however, which seems to be glorifying itself at the expense of school unity, and I think that can only be harmful in the long run."

"Can you name this club?" I asked, wondering if he'd have the guts to challenge me face to face.

"No," he said, and then he paused dramatically to turn from the camera to me, "but I believe *you* can, Mr. Durant."

The interview ended suddenly as the student director signaled that we'd run out of time, which meant I didn't get a chance to deliver a comeback. I didn't think it was that big a deal, though, until I started getting ragged on about the dig in my next class. And the one after that. And so on, for the next few days. Attendance at the next Radical Wave meeting was down from the week before, and fewer people were wearing their Wave colors. Janet started giving me pitying looks when our paths crossed, which made me kind of sick.

But the tide turned again when I interviewed Mike Geier, commissioner of education. The whole time he was in the studio, he looked at the cameras as if they were going to attack him. I asked Mike to describe his job, and it gradually became clear that he didn't have a clue about it. He talked about school spirit, he talked about the importance of getting good grades, and he even talked about our football team's first victory of the season, but he completely avoided my question. Then he concluded: "There's nothing more important than a good education, if you ask me, and I think many students come to Westport High expecting one. It's a good thing they do, because if we lose our minds in high school, we may never get them back. We can't let that happen." He smiled triumphantly.

Even the jaded camera operators were grinning and shaking their heads. "Well, Mike, I can't argue with you there," I admitted. "Nobody should have to lose his mind if he doesn't want to. But let's get back to the central issue here. What is it you *do* as commissioner of education?" I turned back to the camera and smiled the way I'd seen network correspondents do when they went in for the kill.

Mike discussed his involvement in poster-making and other campus activities and praised the job David Whitworth was doing as president, but he continued to evade my question. Finally, in desperation, he said, "I guess I try to be a model student in a way— you know, to set an example for others."

Now he'd stepped in it. "Well, Mike, that is really admirable. Could you tell our audience what your GPA is, just to give us all a little inspiration?"

"No," he said, getting red-faced, "that's personal."

"Fair enough. How about giving us a run-down on the courseload you're carrying?"

His face reddened some more and he said, "That's personal, too."

"Well," I said, "I certainly respect your Fifth Amendment right not to incriminate yourself, Mike, but how can we follow your example if you refuse to talk about your own education?"

It took a minute for the implications of my question to register, and then he leaned over, grabbed me by the collar, and started to say awful things about my mother.

Mr. Armitage, the audiovisual coordinator, burst out of the control room and pulled Mike off me before I had a chance to defend my mother's honor. It wasn't a live broadcast, so Mr. Armitage made us cut the last part of the tape, after settling for an apology from Mike.

"You could go all the way as a TV reporter, T.J.," Mr. Armitage told me when class ended that day.

Mike's outburst never aired, but the rest of the broadcast did, and soon posters began to appear around campus with messages like LOST MIND—REWARD IF RETURNED UNDAMAGED and GUESS MIKE GEIER'S GPA AND WIN

147

VALUABLE CASH PRIZES! Mike started to keep a very low profile, and David Whitworth ran a message in the morning bulletin in which he defended his friend against "vicious, unfair rumors and criticisms," saying that without Mike Geier's work as commissioner, "the educational climate at this school would be very stormy indeed."

For several days after that, David and Mike were tormented virtually everywhere they went by students imitating the sounds of thunder, howling wind, and torrential rain. It got so bad that Dean Phelps finally came on the public-address system for morning announcements and called for an end to "gratuitous, disruptive sound effects and noise-making during and between classes."

Students backed off, but the point had been made: Apathy at Westport High was on the decline, and students were going to start holding their leadership council members accountable for their actions.

On a Friday evening in early November, the thirty Radical Wave members with the best sales records were invited to attend a banquet at the Ocean View Senior Center, where Stella Van Zant, the manager, was going to accept a $4,723 check from our club. After putting on a suit and tie and marveling at the stranger in the bathroom mirror, I walked over to Vivian's house. She emerged wearing a mouth-watering red taffeta dress, a pearl necklace, and red enamel earrings shaped like peace signs.

We walked to a local park, sat down on a bench, and got into some heavy-duty kissing for a while. Vivian's dress rustled whenever she made the slightest movement, and she smelled like a mountain meadow after a summer rain shower. *This* was heaven.

"We'll be late," she whispered when we came up for air. She was lying against my shoulder with her eyes closed and a big grin on her face.

I kissed one of her dimples and said, "They'll wait. I've got the check."

She laughed, opened her remarkable eyes, and said, "You know, if I'm not careful, I just might fall in love with you."

"Worse things could happen to a girl," I said as I kissed her neck.

She pushed me away and said, "*Au contraire, mon cher*. A guy on the rebound is often the worst thing that can happen to a girl. I know the risks I'm taking here, and I'm not complaining yet, but I am curious: Where exactly do things stand with us right now?"

"I never even look at other women anymore," I joked.

Vivian's eyes narrowed with anger and hurt, she pushed me completely away, and sat up straight. She pulled a hand mirror out of her purse and began busily touching up her hair.

"Vivian, I was kidding," I began apologetically, but then I was cut off by a look that would have cowed a charging grizzly bear.

"If only you were," she said coldly. "I see the way you still salivate over Janet when your paths cross at school! There are limits to my patience, and you're reaching them, sport." She paused and studied my face carefully. I tried to look as sorry as I felt. "Besides," she said, starting to show just a hint of a smile, "leading a girl on is not polite."

"Forgive me, Ms. Manners!" I pleaded, and when she laughed, the tension between us eased a few notches. We stood and began to walk toward the center. I could hardly blame Vivian for getting ticked at me. She'd climbed way out on a limb and as much as said that she was in love with me, and I'd left her hanging! What a dork I was! I needed to have my head examined.

The senior center was a nondescript white stucco building that afforded a terrific view of an ugly gray cluster of offshore oil platforms. Inside the center, the dining area had been laid out with gold-colored paper tablecloths, blue paper napkins, blue Styrofoam plates, and white plastic cups, knives, forks, and spoons. (We appreciated the use of our school colors, and we knew that if the seniors had had the money for a *fancy* banquet, they wouldn't have needed our help in the first place.) Vivian and I quickly located Alex, who was proudly showing off his polka-dot clip-on tie. Robin was looking splendid in a powder blue dress with puffed sleeves. Alex pointed out some of the more notable sights in the room: Sandbar Sam bursting out of a tuxedo; Spider Martinez, his hair combed *back* from his face, being hugged and bragged about by his effervescent grandmother; and Dizzy Danny Donahue, who'd actually managed to wear a *clean* white T-shirt for a change.

I felt a tap on my shoulder, then heard the familiar question: "Broken any laws yet, boy?"

I turned around and hugged Grandpa Hensley, who appeared to be all dressed up for a round of golf—on Mars. "Not yet, Grandpa," I replied. "I didn't know golf pants came in that shade of orange, by the way."

He laughed, and then he got the usual gleam in his eyes. Before he could ask me about condoms, though, I introduced him to Robin, reintroduced him to Vivian, and let Alex speak for himself. Grandpa kissed both Robin and Vivian and then told them, "Two lovely ladies like yourselves should know better than to hang out with such unrepentant degenerates."

Alex retaliated by asking Grandpa where he'd gotten his magenta blazer waxed, and the old guy practically laughed himself into a coma. "I'll have to tell that one to Grandma! She *hates* this blazer!" he crowed with delight.

"Where is Grandma, by the way?" I wondered.

The question sobered him up a little. "Oh, she'll be along," he said, grinning puckishly. "Let me show you kids to your table." I knew that grin—Grandpa was up to something. But as hard as I tried, I couldn't pump any information out of him. He put Vivian, Alex, and me in reserved seats at the head table and seated Robin at a table just across from us so that she and Alex "could still make goo-goo eyes at each other."

While Grandpa went to get us some soft drinks, Alex said, "My mom is real proud of me these days, and I have you to thank for it, bud. I get a few students from the Wave to help wipe out the graffiti around the trailer park, and before you know it my neighbors are all telling her what a hero her son is."

"That's great! . . . But don't thank me," I said as I took hold of Vivian's hand. "This woman started it all with an inspiring tale of cookies and lemonade."

Vivian smiled brightly, tugged self-consciously at an earring, and began to accuse me of oversimplifying things, but she was interrupted by a sudden commotion at the back of the dining room. We looked up and saw Grandma Hensley—accompanied by Dr. Fremont, Mr. Horton, Stella Van Zant, and my parents and sisters—leading a TV news crew toward the front table. A *real* TV news crew.

As the crowd started to cheer and I quickly clued into what this would mean, I bolted from my chair and ran up to hug my wonderful grandmother. "Thank you," I whispered as I held her tightly. "Thank you so much."

"You deserve it, honey," she whispered back. "God bless you." She kissed me on the cheek, and then I was surrounded by my beaming family. My mother and sisters kissed me, and my dad shook my hand and grinned as he congratulated me on "doing the family proud."

The next few minutes passed by as if in a dream. As the Rad Wavers continued to cheer wildly, the cameramen got into position and I was guided to the podium with Alex and Vivian to present the check to Ms. Van Zant. Ms. Van Zant, looking like a senator with her carefully coiffed platinum hair and a chin that looked sharp enough to cut diamonds, said in a low, elegant voice, "While the name of your group is rather unorthodox, your actions on behalf of your school and community speak for themselves. This money, combined with other donations, will finally enable us to complete the equipment purchases for our activities center. You have shown us all what good young people can do when they set their minds to it." She asked the Wave members in the audience to stand up and come forward, and

154

when everyone was assembled in the front of the room, the seniors rose and gave us a thunderous standing ovation.

"What a rush!" a wide-eyed Dizzy Danny yelled, and that brought the house down.

Dr. Fremont, Mr. Horton, and the club officers were interviewed afterward. Dr. Fremont, a trim, copper-haired man with tired but friendly blue eyes and a ready smile, pointed out that our club projects were completely student-initiated, which showed "what great young people we have at Westport High. We will continue to support them in any way we can."

Mr. Horton whipped off his sunglasses, looked grimly at the camera, and said, "The future belongs to the young. Do we have the courage to turn and follow in their footsteps or shall we continue our relentless avaricious march to the yawning abyss of narcissistic despotism? *Think* about it, people, before it's too late."

The on-air reporter quickly jerked the microphone away from Mr. Horton, smiled uneasily at the camera, and said, "And that's the good news from Westport Beach. Back to you, Stan."

The rest of the dinner was a total jolt. After

that fantastic kickoff, nobody seemed to mind the soggy salad, the rubber lasagna, or the runny green Jell-O. We all couldn't wait to get home to watch ourselves on TV.

Vivian, Alex, Robin, and I watched the news at Alex's trailer. (He had called his mom to tell her to watch at work.) We impatiently suffered through the headlines . . . the sports . . . and then the weather. We all groaned as the weatherman promised "classic" Santa Ana conditions for the weekend. (The Santa Ana was a hot, dry wind that roared out of the local mountains in the fall and stirred up all kinds of trouble.)

Time was running out. "Maybe we've been cut," Alex said, giving me a worried look.

"Don't give up yet!" Robin said nervously as she leaned against him and squeezed his arm.

Robin called it right—we were on next. "Teen activism is not dead, at least not in the seaside community of Westport Beach," the reporter began. My stomach began to tap-dance on my intestines. I hadn't expected it to be so hard to watch myself on TV. I thought I looked smaller and paler and more nervous on the tube than I did in real life. My eyes looked gray instead of blue, and my sandy brown hair was standing up a little in the back. (Worst of all, the zit on my chin was so obvious, just screaming for attention. What a disaster!) It seemed unfair that Vivian and Alex looked so great by comparison.

I quickly realized, though, that Alex and Vivian must have been stressing over similar thoughts because they, like me, covered their faces and moaned when their images appeared on-screen. Ms. Van Zant looked like she was going to break into a political speech at any moment, and Dr. Fremont gave the impression he was selling toothpaste. And I had to admit, Mr. Horton looked remarkably like a vampire, especially when he arched his eyebrow and said "yawning abyss." The reporter kept calling our club the "*Ridical* Wave." But hey, how could we complain? The segment was three glorious minutes long, and it made the Wave look like a first-class operation.

Ten I slept in late the next morning, and woke up to a slew of congratulatory phone calls, including a few from local newspapers. This was all getting pretty heady!

And then Janet called. "Are you busy?" she asked.

"Swamped," I said coldly. "What can I do for you?"

"You don't have to be so formal," she said, sounding a little hurt.

"Give me a break! You avoid me like the plague for almost two months, and now you're slamming *me* for my bad manners? You've got some nerve, chickie babe—"

"Okay, okay. I'm *sorry*. Look, I just called to say that I saw you on TV last night and I was really impressed. You spoke like a pro, and you really looked handsome in that suit. . . . The changes you've gone through in these past few months are just amazing to me, T.J. . . . I mean, you're not just someone's campaign manager anymore. You're a *leader*."

A warm feeling cascaded from my right ear down through the rest of my body and sloshed around in my toes. "Well, thanks, but I hardly did it alone. Alex and *Vivian*," I paused, "and a lot of other people deserve at least as much credit as I do."

"Yeah, but it was your idea. My mother thought you had remarkable presence in front of the camera, by the way."

Janet's voice was like the purr of one of those ridiculously elegant cats that sleep on silk pillows and eat off fine china. I still loved listening to it. "Your mother said something nice about me?"

"Yeah, and she thinks that perhaps it's time for me to join your Radical Wave. I totally agree with her."

Wow! Janet was going to join the Wave? On her *mother's* recommendation? Things were going just the way I'd planned! Before Vivian came along, anyway. "Well, of course you're welcome to become a member. Everyone is," I said with a sudden sense of caution.

"Hey, don't knock yourself out with enthusiasm or anything," Janet said peevishly.

"I'm sorry," I said, "but we're not a red-carpet kind of club." There was a long silence. "Okay," I admitted, "I'd *love* it if you'd join." Who wouldn't? Janet was creative, a hard worker, and she had a lot of clout on campus.

159

She could do the Wave a lot of good. "But won't David get on your case?" I asked as his hateful profile entered my thoughts.

Janet made a disgusted sound and said, "He doesn't have me on a *leash*, T.J., in spite of what everyone seems to think. Besides, I've started thinking ahead to next year and beyond, and it occurred to me while I was watching you last night that you and I would make a terrific team on the council."

"*What?*"

"Don't sound so shocked. You've got the *gift*. Think about it: T.J. Durant, junior class representative . . . and then, who knows? Maybe student body vice-president."

My mind reeled at the prospect. I'd never in my wildest dreams expected this! Even "Dana the Perfect" had never been on the Student Leadership Council! "Well, I . . . I don't know what to say. . . . Thank you!"

Janet laughed and asked, "Do you think Vivian would mind?"

Vivian! I got sort of panicky for a moment and then thought, well, if Vivian really cares for me, she'll be happy about this. "No, she won't mind at all," I said. And then I added impulsively, "Besides, she doesn't have *me* on a leash, either."

We both laughed and chatted about our political futures for a while. Just before she hung up, Janet said, "And let's stop being strangers at school, okay?"

"That'd be great. Thanks for calling."

I put the phone aside and floated up to cloud nine. The Radical Wave had carried me a lot farther than I'd ever expected it to, that was for sure! I looked around my bedroom and marveled at how much it had changed in just the last few minutes. My clipper-ship models looked statelier, somehow, and my desk and bookcase looked positively *presidential*!

By the time the phone rang again, I was already doing some hard-core brainstorming for my spring campaign.

"Hi," Vivian said. "Who've you been talking to? You promised to call me by ten, and that was almost an hour ago. I've been trying to call you, but the line's been busy the whole time."

"Oh, um . . . I unhooked the phone, and then I overslept," I explained.

"Uh-huh," she said, sounding unconvinced. "Well, the Santa Anas really have kicked up, so it's no good for sailing this afternoon like we planned. You still want to get together or are you hoping to *sleep* some more?"

She sounded awfully suspicious. Women's intuition was a spooky thing. "Why don't you come on over and we'll play some discs and think cool thoughts," I suggested.

"I'm there," she said.

Vivian arrived at my now-empty house wearing cutoffs, a pink halter-top, pink thongs, B-52 bomber earrings, and a bright smile. Her skin was moist with sweat. "It's a scorcher," she said when I welcomed her inside.

She looked pretty hot herself. We kissed, but she cut it short.

"Is there anything wrong?" I asked as I glanced nervously at her earrings.

"I'm thirsty," she said, taking my arm and guiding me into my own kitchen. We checked out the refrigerator and decided to make root-beer floats. We took two frosted mugs out of the freezer, and Vivian put two generous scoops of vanilla ice cream into each one. I poured in the root beer, and we both laughed as we slurped quickly to keep the foam under control. Once the foam was taken care of, the floats went down cool and easy. We went into my room, kicked back, listened to some CDs, and talked about what a gas last night had been.

After we finished our floats, Vivian leaned back in my desk chair and rested her fine, tan legs on my cluttered desktop. I kicked back on my bed and absentmindedly admired her body as I held the still-cool mug against my cheek.

"So tell me," Vivian said as she tossed her head back and ran her fingers through her long, dark hair. "What'd you and Janet talk about on the phone this morning?"

My room suddenly felt very small and very hot. "How did you know—"

"Guys are *stupid*," Vivian told my bedroom window. "And they console themselves by assuming that girls are even *stupider*."

Cornered, I apologized for lying and dutifully described the phone call. I should have known what would happen next: Vivian lost it.

She pulled her legs off the desk and swiveled around to face me. "Promises of glory from the girl who dumped you—*for David Whitworth*," Vivian said. "Just like *that*!" The snap of her fingers sounded like the crack of a whip.

"She didn't dump me," I said testily. My head was beginning to ache from the heat. I reached up to push my bedroom window open all the way only to discover that it already *was* open all the way. "God, it's stuffy in here."

Vivian turned away from me and shook her head. "I can't believe that after all she put you through—and after all *we've* been to each other these past two months—that you're still at the beck and call of Princess Barbie. *I just can't believe it!*"

"Calm down, Viv," I said, getting alarmed. "It's not what you think at all! Janet and I are just friends now, I swear. You're not being fair—"

"*Fair!*" Vivian shouted as she stood. "*I'm* not being fair? But it was okay for you to jerk me around while you waited to see if Janet would give you the nod and welcome you back into the high school royal circle? You're *scum*, T.J., of the lowest kind. A pathetic, conniving, brown-nosing scum with delusions of grandeur. You and Janet Brooks *deserve* each other!"

She blew out of my room like a tropical storm and was out of my house before my stunned self could catch up with her.

"It's not what you think, Vivian!" I

shouted out the front door as she ran down the driveway.

But she tore down the street without even looking back.

I was sulking over my fourth consecutive root-beer float when Alex called to ask if Vivian and I wanted to do pizza that night. I told him no and explained.

"You're not really going to run for council, are you?" he asked, sounding deeply concerned.

" '*Et tu, Brute?*' What would be so terrible about having me on the council, anyway?" I replied miserably.

"It's just not *you*, T.J. At least, it's not who you *used* to be. You know, the social critic. The hell-raiser. The champion of the dispossessed—"

"Come on! Give me some credit here. Being on the council wouldn't change me."

After a long pause Alex said, "I won't waste my time arguing with you about this subject again. But I think you're an idiot to let Vivian go for a weasel like Janet. Vivian's the best thing that's ever happened to you."

"But Vivian isn't gone, Alex! I'm sure we'll patch things up! And gosh, it's awful nice to

165

know that even my best friend thinks I've turned into a jerk."

"They say once you admit it, you can be helped," Alex said evenly.

After he hung up, I tossed back the rest of my root-beer float and thought glumly about the high price of success.

Eleven

Mr. Duke Walton gave the class a menacing look and announced: "The driving task is not to be taken lightly. Stop. Look. Listen. Seat belts on. Doors locked."

Mr. Walton taught his driver's ed class the same way he coached the junior varsity volleyball team—loudly. He was a short, bullet-shaped man with a shiny bald head and narrow, dark eyes who'd been blown out of the Oklahoma panhandle by a tornado and who'd just happened to land at Westport High. That was the rumor, anyway.

"Okay, start your cars!" he shouted, as if he were on the line at Indy.

We turned the keys in our shiny white simulators, each of which consisted of a black vinyl seat, a dashboard, a steering wheel, two side-view mirrors, a brake pedal, and an accelerator pedal. (The equipment did *not* include a radio/cassette player or air-conditioning. This school was too cheap for words.) We began to "drive" through the film being shown on the screen at the front of the classroom, while Mr. Walton monitored our progress at a console adjacent to the screen.

"Number fifteen, you just ran a stop sign!" he bellowed. "You're out!"

How many of us would make it through the film today without crashing and burning? It was the kind of excitement that made high school worth all the hassle.

Vivian was driving on my right, her eyes fixed on the screen, her feet carefully braking and accelerating in perfect synchronization with the events in the film. She was obviously going to be an A-1 driver.

"Number three, that was a pedestrian you just ran over!" Mr. Walton screamed.

I leaned toward Vivian. "Nice day for a drive, huh?"

"Watch out!" she said, and we both swerved in time to avoid a dog crossing the street. Numbers six, eleven, twelve, and twenty-seven were not so fortunate.

"Keep your eyes on the road, bozo," Vivian scolded.

I faced the screen again but continued to talk to her. "You saved my life, Viv. Does this mean I'm forgiven, at long last?"

"I'm sure I don't know what you're talking about," she said as we came to a stop at a busy intersection.

"*Number two, you're over the limit line!*"

"I mean an entire week of the silent treatment. I mean treating Janet like she was something the cat dragged in, instead of sophomore class president."

We crossed through the intersection and came to a freeway on ramp.

"Number four, Number twenty, you don't look like a car pool to me! You're in the wrong lane!"

"Those two-bit titles really impress you a lot, don't they, T.J.? Is *Madame President* coming to our beach barbecue this evening?" she asked with acid sweetness.

"There you go again!" I said. The car-pool lane light turned green, and Vivian floored her accelerator. I floored mine, too. She wasn't going to get away from me that easily.

"Numbers eight and fourteen, *ease up*," Mr. Walton said, referring to Vivian and me. "This isn't a drag race."

We both eased up but only a little. Freeway traffic was light at first, but there was a large group of cars bunched up ahead. "Well, is she coming or not?" Vivian persisted. "I'd hate to have her miss out on the fun after all the work she's done for the club."

"Wolf pack ahead! Leave yourself an out!" Mr. Walton warned us.

"You're being sarcastic, right? Well, for your information, Janet is bringing David Whitworth with her."

"Swell," Vivian said as she accelerated again. "I'm sure the three of you will have *lots* to talk about. Why don't you just hand the Wave over to the leadership council on a silver platter and get it over with?"

I sped up, too. Neither of us was paying attention to the stalled car sitting about a quarter of a mile ahead of us. "That's not fair, I—" I stopped talking and slammed on my brakes, remembering too late that accelerating into a stalled car is *not* good driving technique.

"Numbers eight and fourteen, y'all just crashed and burned!" Mr. Walton said with a hint of glee in his voice. He really loved his job.

"Thanks *loads*, T.J.," Vivian said, glaring at me.

"It was *your* fault!"

"Don't make me laugh. If you stopped lusting after Janet Brooks for just ten seconds and tried to get a life, you'd realize that she's only in the Wave now because we got on the

TV news. Suddenly the Wave is popular, and she just couldn't stand to be left out."

"That's not true! You're just jealous of her," I said.

"Have you lost your mind?! Janet and I couldn't be *less* alike, which only goes to show how screwed up your head is these days. But she can have you, sport. At this point, if I had to choose between a math test and a date with you, I'd take the math test!"

Vivian and I were startled by sudden, widespread applause. "He's down for the count, Vivian," a girl yelled.

Several guys encouraged me to get back up and fight.

We were so into our argument that we'd forgotten where we were. But Mr. Walton hadn't. He wanted to see us after class.

"Only five students made it through the simulation today, and I believe that a large part of the blame rests with you two," he told us solemnly after the rest of the class had filed out the door. "You're going to come in after school today and run through it again."

"But we have a barbecue—" I started to say.

"Don't push it, boy," he said ominously. His hands were as large as baseball mitts, so I decided to heed his warning. Vivian and I left driver's ed and walked to English class without saying anything to each other. I was so ticked at her that I didn't care if she ever spoke to me again.

A note from Janet was passed to me while I was studying for the weekly vocabulary test. Janet wasn't even *in* my English class, so I figured the note must be pretty important.

It read: *"Please meet me at lunch in the balcony above the auditorium. Urgent!"*

Yup, *definitely* an emergency.

As class dragged on, everybody was talking to me about the barbecue, but by then it was the last thing on my mind. Janet and Vivian. Vivian and Janet. Did they *have* to be mutually exclusive? Every now and then I sneaked a look at Vivian, who was studying with her friends Stephanie Ashbrook and Lea Bradford. Vivian never looked up, so I couldn't guess what she might have been thinking, although I was pretty sure she wasn't any more interested in the vocabulary test than I was. Stephanie, an intense, thoughtful type who wrote interesting (but violent) poetry for the school literary magazine, caught my eye.

She gave me one of the dirtiest looks I'd ever seen. I could imagine her next poem:

> *A wretched boy betrays my friend*
> *And breaks her heart in two.*
> *Shall we beat the wretched boy*
> *Until he's black and blue?*

Tortured by my conscience, I sped over to the auditorium at the sound of the lunch bell and found Janet waiting in the balcony. She looked sort of down, too.

"What light on yonder balcony breaks?" I said as I approached her. "Tonight we feast, yet Janet is bummed."

She laughed halfheartedly. "If Shakespeare were alive, he'd sue you for butchering his dialogue," she said.

"But he *is* alive," I told her. "I read at the grocery store that he's in Vegas writing songs for Elvis impersonators."

She laughed again and shook her head. "Don't believe everything you read at grocery stores," she advised.

We sat down and looked out over the dark, vacant auditorium. The stage was empty, except for the ghostlike memories of past plays and assemblies.

"So what's so urgent?" I asked.

173

"David gave me an ultimatum," she said with a mixture of anger and indignation. "If I stay in the Radical Wave, our relationship is over."

I was stunned.

She turned to me and said, "He's so jealous of you it's pathetic. All the attention you've been getting lately is just *killing* him, but I think it's wonderful." She leaned forward, kissed me on the lips, and then backed off and flashed her campaign smile at me. "So I told him to take a hike."

I gazed into her mesmerizing blue eyes and my head began to swim. What a bizarre day I was having!

"So what does this mean?" I asked.

"It means that if the rumors are true about you and Vivian breaking up, then I'd be happy to be your, um, partner at the barbecue tonight." She kissed me again, and I kissed her back. When the kiss ended, she sighed and laid her head on my shoulder. "I take it that's a yes," she purred.

I nodded. After all, I'd had no better offers.

"I'm having the weirdest day," I told Alex as we worked on systems of simultaneous equations in math class.

"I know. Vivian told Robin and me all about it at lunch today."

The three of them were talking about me at lunch?! "And I suppose you're taking her side?"

"Why do you suppose *that*, T.J.?" Alex said as he punched some numbers into his calculator.

He had a point. Paranoia was the first sign of a guilty conscience. "So what does she want?" I asked, totally frustrated.

Alex peered up at me over the rims of his glasses and said with mock seriousness, "She desperately wants to be the mother of your children." We both busted out laughing but stopped when the teacher fined us five points each.

"Seriously," I whispered as I pretended to go back to work.

"Okay," he whispered back as he crunched some numbers, "I'll give it to you straight. She wants—we all want—you to come back from your ego trip. We miss you."

"My ego trip!" I blurted. My outburst cost me twenty-five points, and I was ordered to sit in an isolated desk, where I sulked in silence for the rest of the period. Everyone was turning against me!

"You can't fight and drive at the same time!" Mr. Walton told Vivian and me when we reported to him after school.

"But my parents do," I protested. I thought I saw the trace of a smile pass across Vivian's face, which was what I was hoping for. That faint grin was the first response I'd gotten out of her since the morning.

"That's it!" Mr. Walton said, bounding toward my simulator. "Drop and give me twenty!"

"You're kidding," I said, hoping that he was.

He put his face directly in front of mine and said, "Do I *look* like I'm kidding?"

Actually, he looked like he'd been French-kissing the grill of a Mack truck, but I didn't say so. I did twenty push-ups instead, which wasn't easy because Vivian was laughing at me. It was humiliating.

Vivian and I went through the entire simulation in almost total silence, and both of us came through it without so much as a scratched fender. Mr. Walton looked like he wanted to run through the whole thing again but reluctantly decided to release us from custody.

"You've got an attitude problem, boy," he told me as I was leaving.

"I've got nothing *but* problems," I mumbled as I followed Vivian out the door.

Vivian stopped when we entered the hallway, turned-on me, and said sharply, "What, so now you're feeling sorry for yourself?"

I wanted to come back at her with an equally snide remark, but the wind went out of my sails. There was only one thing to say.

"I'm sorry for acting like such a jerk, Viv."

She looked really surprised. "I'm sorry, too," she said quietly. She paused for a moment, and then added, "I guess old friends like us should know better than to try for romance. It ruins everything." The sadness in her eyes made me feel terrible.

"Well, tonight'll be a blast," I said, trying to cheer us both up.

"Yeah," she said, picking up some trash from the hallway floor and tossing it into a nearby garbage can. "A real blast. Listen, T.J., I'll be there tonight as a hostess like I promised, but after that I'm quitting the club."

The news struck me like a bolt of lightning. "Quit? But you can't quit!"

Vivian stuck her right hand on her blue-jeaned hip as if she were reaching for a six-shooter and said, "Who says I can't quit? I can do whatever the hell I want."

"But the Radical Wave needs you!" I said desperately. "You've done at least as much to make it a success as Alex or I have."

"How *nice* of you to notice. But it's way too late for compliments. Besides, I've got a feeling you'll find a replacement for me *real* soon. Everyone knows how resourceful you are."

"What kind of crack is that? Is this about Janet again? How petty can you be!"

"Petty!" she said, outraged. (We had both reached the shouting stage again.) "You're the *expert* on petty. You treat the Wave like it's your own private club, a pet social cause you cooked up to lure back a certain Ocean Avenue princess who changes boyfriends every time her popularity needs a jolt!"

Oooh, that hit below the belt.

Mr. Walton peered out of the doorway and looked at us with wild, disbelieving eyes. "Go home," he pleaded. "Please!"

Vivian started sailing down the hallway under full spinnaker, and I raced after her. "Well if that's the way you really feel about it," I said, struggling to keep my voice down, "then I won't stand in your way."

Vivian turned around for one last shot. "Try standing in my way, Slick," she said in a shrill whisper, "and I may damage something that even Janet Brooks couldn't fix."

I thought about Vivian's comments later, especially the last one, as I loaded frozen hot dogs into a cooler. Maybe the Radical Wave would be better off without her after all. I certainly was!

Or so I thought.

Twelve More than 200 people came to the barbecue, and it took almost two hours to serve all the food. The Wave purchased the pizza, meat, paper plates, napkins, and utensils—everything else was potluck. People had gone all out, contributing everything from malted-milk balls to Madge Schaefer's tuna surprise. (The tuna dish *stayed* a surprise—even Eric steered clear of his mother's culinary masterpiece.) Everyone porked out except Dizzy Danny, who arrived a few hours late because he forgot which beach the party was on, so he had to explore several before he found the right one. "They all look the same to me, dudes," he explained to his laughing friends.

Triple-thick pizza was a hit all around. We offered several varieties: Canadian bacon and pineapple, pepperoni and bell pepper, sausage and olive, ham and tomato, and, for the brave at heart, a gnarly anchovy number laced with Tabasco sauce. (The anchovy creation disappeared faster than anyone expected it to.) As people ate, the inevitable giant multicolored beach ball made its appearance, bouncing from hand to hand across the beach until it made the fatal mistake of landing in Ryan Carey's spaghetti. Ryan is a thin, moody guy whose body seems to be covered with heavy-metal tattoos. He can be pretty intense even on his best days—so no one was particularly surprised when he whipped out a switchblade, speared the offending beach ball, and then calmly returned to his spaghetti while his victim collapsed and wheezed to its death.

When we ran out of pizza we cooked hot dogs, and when we ran out of hot dogs we toasted some chocolate marshmallow meltdowns. There was enough soda around to fill a good-sized swimming pool. (It was a good thing, too—Spider's "mucho macho salsa" was setting tongues on fire all over the place.) Portable stereos were tuned into the same station, so those who wanted to could boogie in the sand. The only casualty was Eric Roos, who took one on the chin when he made the mistake of pulling the string on Stacy Reynoso's bikini top. Nobody could blame Stacy for wanting to deck him, but almost everyone thought she overdid it when she tried to stomp on his neck.

Some nice wave sets were coming in, and

the surfer crowd had noticed. The glass-cutters, goofy-footers, and foamsmiths of Westport High were shooting tubes with such radical moves—their bodies illuminated by the pier lights—that crowds gathered to watch and applaud their performances all evening.

Three giant volleyball games got under way, and a group of guys squared off against a group of girls in a major kite battle. The girls won when their California condor kite forced the guys' screaming eagle kite out of the sky and into the briny deep. "That would never happen for *real*," one of the guys protested afterward. The girls laughed.

Vivian kept pretty much to herself and, true to her word, left as soon as the food lines died down. She wouldn't stay to eat, and she didn't so much as look at me. Alex and Robin basically treated Janet like a dead fish and kept giving me scornful looks. They finally ditched us and strolled down the beach together to read some poetry and catch the sunset. Too rude!

"Alex has never liked me, has he?" Janet asked forlornly after they'd left.

I put my arm around her and said, "Give him time. He'll come around." She gave me an uncertain look, and then I kissed her. She smiled gratefully and challenged me to race her to the water. I ran after her, admiring her outstanding black one-piece, which was split in front by a white lightning bolt zigzagging from her left hip to her right shoulder. We splashed each other and laughed and dodged waves for a while, as the sun began to set and the unseasonable heat began to let up a little. It seemed so natural to be playing in the surf with Janet—it felt like summer again. Actually, it was even *better* than last summer because we were more like equals now. She didn't just want me as a campaign manager anymore—she wanted me as a running mate!

About a half-hour after sunset, Sandbar Sam gathered everyone together to toast the Wave. "This is just the beginning of an amped-up year! So party hearty, dudes and dudettes!" he said, raising his soda can into the air.

The crowd roared its approval. "And let's give credit where credit is due, to our radical officers: T.J., Alex, and the most bodacious Vivian!" Sam continued. The crowd cheered even louder, but I was the only club officer around to cheer back.

"What's the hap, T.J.?" Sam asked. "Where's Alex and my babe Vivian? She didn't bail on us, did she? Yo, Vivian!" he yelled. (I was pretty sure I heard the windows rattle on nearby beach houses. Sam had that kind of voice.)

Everybody looked at me expectantly, and Janet stared self-consciously at her toes. "They went out to buy a keg of Pepto-Bismol," I said, and the crowd laughed so hard that Alex and Vivian were temporarily forgotten. But I was starting to feel pretty rotten about the way things were turning out. They both should've been here to enjoy this moment with me.

Later, as Janet and I huddled together next to a huge bonfire, I looked into the flames and saw Vivian's dimpled, skeptical face. She'd given me advice on how to get "in with the *in* crowd," and the moment it started to work, she blew up on me. The girl really was *perverse*. I sure missed her, though. And Alex . . . how could *he* turn on me? We'd been best friends since the sixth grade, and now he was taking Vivian's side!

I angrily shoved them out of my mind and pulled Janet close. "You were great to come," I said. "I'm having the best time."

She sighed happily and lay her head against my chest. "I missed you a lot, too, T.J." I stroked her hair until she sat up, turned to me, and asked, "But I do have one question.

What did you *see* in Vivian Chandler?! I mean, frankly, I can't understand the attraction. She's so *moody*, and out of it, and the clothes she wears are just—"

"I don't want to talk about Vivian," I said sharply.

"Well, excuse *me*," Janet said, getting all offended. I quickly apologized because I knew if I didn't she'd get real pouty.

"That's okay," she said. "I guess I can't blame you for being a little edgy tonight. It's not every club that gets abandoned by its officers in the middle of a major party."

I glared into her flickering blue eyes and said, "Vivian *quit* the Wave this afternoon, okay? She came tonight precisely because she didn't want to leave us in the lurch."

"*Oh* . . . so, um, who's going to take over the club for you *next* year? Alex?"

The question stunned me. "What are you talking about? I started this club—why would I let someone else run it for me?"

"But you can't do this *and* be on the council."

"Sure I can!"

Janet laughed and shook her pretty blond head. "You obviously have no idea how time-consuming council is."

"And he never will, if I can help it," said a drunken voice behind us. Janet and I turned and were amazed to see David Whitworth standing—more like swaying, really—behind us.

"David! What are *you* doing here?" Janet asked. It was clear that she wasn't totally unhappy to see him.

"I've come to save you from yourself," he said, staggering closer to the fire.

"Don't breathe on the flames," I warned as I stepped between him and the fire. "You could kill us all."

Janet regarded David with a look of disgust. "You're drunk."

He shook his head. "I've only had eight—no, *nine* beers," he said indignantly, letting out a mongo belch.

"You'd better leave before you make an even bigger fool of yourself," I said. "No booze at this party. City ordinance. You remember all about rules and ordinances, don't you?" People started to come over from other bonfires to see what all the commotion was about.

"Don't lecture *me*, you little punk," David said as he stumbled toward me, except that he ended up staggering into Sandbar Sam instead.

"Yo, Prez!" Sam said. "Your breath is killing the palm trees. Too many brewskis?"

David shot him a look of contempt. "Out of my way, you lousy Polynesian moron." The crowd gasped, but Sam took the slam in stride.

"Too many brewskis," Sam said, shaking his head and throwing David over his shoulder as if he were a beach towel. With David dangling down his back, Sam marched purposefully toward the water and we all followed.

As Sam began to walk into the surf, Janet panicked and screamed, "Don't drown him! He didn't mean what he said! He's an idiot when he's drunk!"

"Chill out, woman," Sam told her calmly as he dunked David into the surf a few times. "I'm just giving him the moronic Polynesian cure for drunkenness."

David came out of his "shower" looking a whole lot more alert. "Why'd you do that?" he asked Sam in a bewildered voice as they returned to dry land.

"Because you asked for it," Sam said good-naturedly.

"I did?" David looked around at the large

crowd of students and began to get an idea of the situation he'd put himself in. Even I felt a little bad for him. He looked as sorry as a wet kitten.

Janet gave him a pitying look and gently guided him to one of the fire pits. "For the first time in my life, I feel like a loser," he told her. "I never thought you'd come to this party after I asked you not to. Especially to be with *him*," he said, gesturing at me with his thumb.

"This is a rerun, David. I *loathe* reruns," Janet reminded him as her pity evaporated into the fire-heated air. "Maybe you'd better go home now."

"But I miss you," he said pathetically, dropping to his knees and embracing her legs. "I *love* you."

"This is *so* embarrassing," she said, looking to me for help.

I rounded up a few volunteers to escort David home, but he stood and declared that he could make it on his own. Once we were sure he hadn't driven to the beach, we decided not to press the issue. He gave Janet one last chance to leave with him, but she declined.

He turned to me just before he left and said quietly, "You may've won this battle,

Durant, but the war ain't over 'till the surrender papers are signed."

"Are you *sure* you had only nine beers?" I asked him, but he just snickered and began to stagger home.

"What did he mean, 'the war ain't over?' " I asked Janet.

"He's drunk," she said as she watched his departure with a mixture of pity and contempt. "Don't pay attention to anything he says."

The revelers returned to their bonfires, but David's ugly visit had cast a pall over the festivities, and pretty soon the party began to disintegrate.

I walked Janet to her house, trying unsuccessfully to engage her in conversation. She'd gotten real quiet after David left, and I was afraid of what she might be thinking. "David must be really crazy about you, to come to the beach and make a fool of himself that way," I said, desperately hoping she'd disagree with me.

But she smiled dreamily and said, "Yeah." Then she snapped out of it and said, "But of course, I had a wonderful time with *you* tonight, T.J. . . . although, to be honest, I think we really are better off as friends, don't you?"

I nodded. It really had been just a summer romance, after all.

"I still meant what I said about us running together for council this spring," she said brightly. But then she bit her lip and added, "Of course, you really will have to make some choices, you know?"

I nodded again, thinking with disgust that I'd been making nothing but *bad* choices lately. "I'll need to think it over," I told her. We stared at each other awkwardly for a while, and said good night at her doorstep. There was really nothing else to say.

I took the long way home, following the dreary, treeless San Miguel River trail, which afforded a spectacular view of the regional power station. The plant, which was huge, gray, and featureless by daylight, looked pretty creepy at night, with its brightly illuminated entrails and its dark towers topped by ominous red beacons. Maybe if I jumped into the river (which consisted, for most of the year, of tidal water flow from the sea), I might be sucked into the plant through one of its huge cooling valves. My sorry life would end as a brief blip on some technician's screen, which was only fitting for a loser like me. I'd almost gotten Janet out of my heart, but the minute she stroked my ego, I fell for her all over again. Pathetic!

And Vivian hated me now. Vivian! I'd really screwed her over—and for what? It was clear that I didn't deserve her . . . or any other girl. I was the sleaziest, slimiest scum of a guy on the planet Earth.

I worked myself into a self-hating frenzy, vowing I'd never go out with another girl for as long as I lived. I also decided that instead of jumping into the salty San Miguel, I'd go away and die alone and unmourned on that island I'd told Vivian about. I deserved no less for acting like such a bozo.

My only consolation was the certainty that things couldn't get any worse.

Thirteen

"So she really is in love with David Whitworth, and I've been a total jerk, and I'm majorly sorry," I told Alex as we rode our bikes to school on Monday morning.

"Don't be too hard on yourself, dude," Alex said, grinning at my apology. "I haven't exactly been Mr. Wonderful. Robin and I shouldn't have ditched you at the barbecue that way. It was my idea, and it sucked. I just couldn't stand to see you back with Janet, I guess."

"No chance of that now."

"I won't pretend I'm sorry. But look," Alex continued, "if you're really crazy enough to want to run for council, I'll help you out with that. After all, I did it for Big Wave Dave."

I steered my bike closer to his, and we exchanged a high-five. "Thanks, bud," I said. "I'm still thinking through the pros and cons, but it's nice to know I'll have you on my side if I decide to go for it."

As we turned the corner at Palm and Central, the Westport High tower came into view. No matter how I felt about going to school on any particular day, the sight of the tower was always inspiring. And today, on a cool, blue, November morning, it looked especially nice.

But as we got closer to the school, I noticed there was something different about the tower. I couldn't pin down the difference at first, but suddenly it became horribly clear: *Graffiti!*

Someone had painted graffiti on the tower! For a Westport High Sea Lion with any spirit at all, seeing graffiti on the tower was like seeing a mustache on the *Mona Lisa*, a bra on the Statue of Liberty, a giant golf ball on top of the Washington Monument!

"I'll round up some Thrashers and we'll wipe it out ASAP," Alex said with disgust before we were even close enough to read the graffiti. "Someday, though, I'd just love to catch a tagger in the act so I could grind his face in it."

Alex came to a screeching halt. "Hang on, partner. That graffiti belongs to us!"

Confused, I came to a stop, followed his gaze, and realized that the graffiti on the tower was readable now. It read: THE RADICAL WAVE RULES AT WESTPORT HIGH!

"Oh my God!" I exclaimed, not wanting to believe my eyes.

We raced to the parking lot, locked our bikes to the rack, and rushed onto campus. There was Radical Wave graffiti everywhere. On the gym. The administration building. The drama building. The language-arts building. The science building. The cafeteria. It was sickening. The school had been hit by graffiti before, but never like this.

My mind reeled as I began to consider what this could mean. The end of my club, embarrassment for my family, the death of my budding political career. *This was a total disaster!*

But it was pretty much a personal disaster. There were a lot of students on campus already, and while a few were out gawking at the damage, most were just kicking back as if all were well in the world. Alex went out on reconnaissance, while I tried to round up club members for an emergency meeting. A few people razzed me as I walked by—cheerleaders and athletes, mostly—but a lot of other students congratulated me on the "artistic statement." I was suddenly getting a terrible headache, and it had "graffiti" sprayed all over it.

Mike Geier came by to laugh in my miserable face. "So much for your wannabe political career, eh, Durant?" he said.

"You did this! You and David!" I shouted as I stormed up to assault him. He easily pushed me away, and I fell flat on my butt.

"Don't you *wish*, dirtbag!" he said with a sneer, and then he laughed and walked off toward the leadership office.

Mike and David were behind this, for sure. The stupid, self-satisfied gleam in Mike's eyes told the whole disgusting story. Of course, he could flaunt it all he wanted, because there was no way I could prove anything. The only evidence in this crime was the name of my club, scrawled everywhere for all the world to see.

I slowly got up, rubbing my sore butt. So David *had* made good on his threats after all. He was going to ruin me, even if he had to trash his own school in the process. The slime!

I eventually located Sam, who was bellowing, "I don't like it!" with the regularity of a fog horn. I enlisted his vocal skills to call an emergency meeting in the quad. A crowd of hard-core members slowly gathered, and soon there was talk of stringing up Mike and David. I had to remind everyone that we had no real evidence—and that the best thing we could do at this point was to concentrate on cleaning up the mess.

Janet came by, took me aside, and told me apologetically that, under the circumstances, it would be impossible for her to stay in the club. "But if there's anything I can do—" she started to say.

"There is," I said angrily. "Get David to 'fess up. I know he and Mike are behind this. Mike is gloating all over the place even as we speak."

"Oh no, T.J.," Janet said, looking shocked. "David couldn't possibly do something like this. Not in a million years! He *loves* this school. It's his whole life. And I can vouch for him because . . . because we were together almost the entire weekend." She blushed, touched my cheek, and whispered, "I'm sorry." And then she walked away.

I knew by the way she said it that our politcal partnership was now every bit as dead as our romance. I was in free-fall, and there was no end in sight.

Teachers and administrators were beginning to walk around the campus to inspect the damage. Dr. Fleming looked at me with profound disappointment in his eyes and said, "I want you in my office by the time the tardy bell rings. You, Vivian, and Alex. Got it?"

I nodded hopelessly as he continued his inspection. A crowd of deans, counselors, and assistant principals followed him, shaking their heads and wringing their hands.

I was stressing out to the max when Vivian appeared. "This must be a *very* happy morning for you," I said bitterly, before she could even open her mouth.

"That's a terrible thing to say, T.J.," she began.

"But I've finally gotten what I *deserve*, haven't I? This'll end my 'ego trip' and cut me back down to size, won't it? And it looks like you left the club just in time, Viv. You won't even have to help clean up the mess I've created."

She shook her head. "But I actually came here to—"

I covered my ears and shouted, "I can't take it this morning, Vivian. I'm wiped out! Dead! *Finished!* Why don't you just go to first period and kick back, while Alex and I go to Fremont's office to face the firing squad."

"You are such an idiot!" she screamed as her eyes filled with tears. "I came here to offer my *help*, but to hell with you! Maybe you do

197

deserve this, after all!" She turned and tore off across the green in the direction of the central locker area.

I felt like a total chump the second she started to cry, but my emotions had gotten so screwed up that I couldn't quite manage to choke out one more apology.

Alex had returned, and he had Robin with him. He watched Vivian's departure and then said to Robin, "T.J. really has a way with girls. I should take notes."

"They even chalked graffiti on the P.E. field," Robin told me as she jabbed Alex with her elbow. "Whoever did this must *really* hate us."

No kidding.

It seemed as if all the power players at Westport High were in Dr. Fleming's plush, blue-and-gold-carpeted office when Alex and I were ushered in. Fleming's mafia, as the administrative staff was sometimes called, all carried walkie-talkies, which distinguished them from the teachers. The walkie-talkies were abuzz with updates on the graffiti damage, as well as with more mundane reports about tardy students, unlocked gates, and missing teachers.

Ms. Elder, a nice lady whose body lacked the strange lumps and curves found on so many other faculty members, and whose enormous blue eyes invited teenage trust, gave Alex and me the hopeless but understanding nod of a veteran counselor. Mr. Ito smiled at us, but it was one of his weaker efforts. Dean Phelps regarded us with a stony glare. Assistant principals Lupe Aguilar and Nick Beeler were busy writing notes on yellow legal pads and didn't even look up at us when we walked in. Campus Police Officer Reggie Dembro didn't look up at us, either. He was too busy adjusting the volume on his walkie-talkie. He couldn't seem to turn it down, and even the static between transmissions was pretty loud—or seemed loud to Alex and me. Everyone else in the office just ignored it.

Dr. Fremont cleared his throat, which seemed to signal the beginning of the meeting. "Gentlemen," he said solemnly, looking at Alex and me, "in the twenty-seven years I have served this district, this is the worst display of student vandalism I have ever witnessed."

"KING SEVEN TO BASE. WE HAVE A FLOODED TOILET IN THE GIRLS' BATHROOM ON THE SECOND FLOOR OF THE LANGUAGE-ARTS BUILDING," Officer Dembro's walkie-talkie screamed. "THERE IS STANDING WATER IN THE HALLWAY."

Everyone turned to look at poor Officer Dembro, who shrugged as he twisted the useless volume control. We heard "Base" (code for the main office staff) dispatch a custodian to investigate the clogged toilet, and Lupe Aguilar excused herself to oversee the cleanup. (I couldn't blame her for wanting to go. A wet and slippery hallway during passing period could mean lawsuit central, especially in a rich beach town like this one.)

"We're talking about thousands of dollars' worth of damage," Dean Phelps said ominously.

"From one toilet?" I asked incredulously.

"Don't get smart with me, Durant," Dean Phelps said. He was a tall thin man with large green eyes, a bold long nose, close-cropped salt-and-pepper hair, out-of-control eyebrows, and a sensible gray suit that looked as if it had been cleaned with Zog's Sex Wax. I'd always had the impression that when other boys were dreaming of becoming cowboys, astronauts, firemen, and presidents, little Darryl Phelps already had his heart set on becoming a high school dean of discipline.

"But why do you assume someone in our

club did this?" I asked. "We love this school. We've gone out of our way to show it by taking graffiti *off* of school walls."

"We know all about the accomplishments of your Radical Wave," Ms. Elder said in her sad but sweet way, "but there's obviously a bad apple in your bunch somewhere."

"An apt metaphor, Ms. Elder," Dr. Fremont said approvingly. How could he think about apt metaphors at a time like this? My whole life was caving in on me!

"We're not accusing your club as a whole of this action, boys, but it is your club's name that's sprayed all over campus, is it not?" Dean Phelps asked in a less accusing tone.

"But we held an emergency meeting this morning," I said, "and nobody in the club did it. *Everyone* will swear to it, if you want."

The adults in the office exchanged smirks and knowing glances. "We think it was sabotage," I continued, starting to feel like a salmon at the base of Niagara Falls.

Dean Phelps and Officer Dembro laughed out loud, and even Dr. Fleming grinned a little. "Seriously, T.J.," Dr. Fleming said, "do you expect us to believe that someone would do this just to sabotage the standing of your club on this campus? I simply don't believe we have that kind of student here at Westport High."

"Who do you think is trying to sabotage your club?" Ms. Elder asked in a more sympathetic tone.

I started to say, but then Alex shook his head at me. Oh yeah—innocent until proven guilty. I needed *proof*. "I guess I'm not sure," I forced myself to admit.

Dr. Fleming nodded in a self-satisfied way.

"KING TEN TO SMOKEY ONE. KING TEN TO SMOKEY ONE. A GUN HAS BEEN FOUND IN THE BOYS' LOCKER ROOM," Officer Dembro's walkie-talkie reported.

Officer Dembro, 250 pounds of sincerity, looked around casually, as if he hadn't heard a thing.

"*You're* Smokey One, Reggie!" Dean Phelps reminded him in an alarmed voice.

Officer Dembro abruptly stood up, excused himself, and rushed out of the room. Nick Beeler followed him. We were now fresh out of assistant principals.

Dr. Fleming, unruffled as ever, turned to Mr. Ito and said, "What do you think, Larry?"

"I'm opposed to bringing guns on campus, of course," Mr. Ito said.

Dr. Fleming loosened his tie and said in a somewhat more agitated voice, "*No*, I mean what do you think about the Radical Wave?"

"Oh, well, I think the Radical Wave has brought a great deal more good to this campus and the community than any of us initially expected it to. But the fact is, some person or persons have obviously taken their affection for this club a little too far."

"Far too far," Dean Phelps agreed, turning up the volume on his walkie-talkie slightly, presumably for updates on the flooded toilet and confiscated gun.

"And so, boys," Dr. Fleming said, "I am afraid that the Radical Wave will have to be suspended indefinitely."

Alex and I exchanged desperate looks. *The death sentence.*

"But we can clean up the graffiti in no time!" Alex protested.

"We'll raise money to pay for the damage!" I offered.

"Well, now that's very admirable of you, boys, of course. But what's to stop this from happening again tomorrow or next week? Try to see the problem from our perspective," Dr. Fleming said. (Why did adults always say that, as if such a thing were possible?)

"But this isn't fair! Under American law, we're innocent until proven guilty," Alex said.

"This isn't America, young man, this is a *high school*," Dean Phelps pointed out. "Having a club on this campus is a privilege, not a right. And when a club causes even one student to go astray, then that club has outlived its usefulness."

"But suppose they can prove that the vandalism was committed by someone from outside the club?" Mr. Horton asked as he entered the principal's office. Alex and I smiled with relief at our club advisor, who was in the process of removing his hat, coat, and sunglasses. We knew he wouldn't let us down.

"Good morning, Ed," an obviously surprised Dr. Fleming said, "We weren't sure you'd be able to make it."

"Hiya, Doc. Actually, nobody told me about this meeting until just a few minutes ago," Mr. Horton explained. (Alex and I had sent a note to him via a student courier.) He turned back to Dean Phelps and said, "Well, what about it, Darryl?"

"Your point is irrelevant, Ed, and you know it. No matter who is actually responsible, if we let the Radical Wave continue after an incident like this, it will send the wrong kind of message to the student body."

"That's not the real problem here," Mr. Horton said as he glared at Dean Phelps. "The bottom line is, you've wanted the Wave to fail all along, because of its name and its apparel and the kind of students it attracts, and now you have the excuse you need to do it in. Forget the money raised for the senior center and other successful projects. Forget the morale boost it's given to hundreds of kids. No, let's shut it down without a trial, without so much as a hearing!"

"You know, Darryl, he's right," Ms. Elder said, smiling at Mr. Horton. "We're doing these boys here an injustice. They should be given a chance to prove their innocence."

Dr. Fleming seemed disturbed by this sudden shift. "But I thought we'd settled this issue, Tammy, we—"

"That's just it! A fine educational leader like yourself resorting to the tactics of a hanging judge!" Mr. Horton said, really getting into it. Mr. Ito and Mr. Phelps looked at him as if he'd flipped out, but Ms. Elder seemed sort of enchanted by his performance. "I will not stand for it! If you wish to trample on our Constitution in front of these young men, then so be it. But I'll fight you on this all the way.

I'll go to the union, I'll go to the board, I'll even go to the *media* if I have to!" Mr. Horton said, shaking his fists with righteous rage.

"I won't stand for it, either," Dean Phelps said, turning to Dr. Fleming. "We can't allow the theatrical whims of one iconoclastic teacher on behalf of one unworthy club to jeopardize the order I—*we*—have brought to this campus."

Dean Phelps was interrupted by a call on his walkie-talkie: "SMOKEY TWO TO KING FOUR. MR. SHOREBURG HAS BEEN LOCKED OUT BY HIS GOVERNMENT CLASS AGAIN. THIS TIME THEY'RE DEMANDING TO SPEAK TO THE SUPERINTENDENT."

"I'll be right there," Dean Phelps said into his walkie-talkie as he shook his head with disgust. Alex and I started to crack up, but then we suppressed it. "You haven't heard the last from me," Dean Phelps told us as he got up to leave the office.

Dr. Fleming was starting to look a little ragged. After the dean left he said, "Listen, boys. I'm a reasonable man. And Mr. Horton here is very persuasive." Mr. Horton, a ham at heart, grinned at the good review. "I'll give you twenty-four hours to come up with concrete evidence that the mess outside was not perpetrated by someone in your club. And in the meantime, I'll take you up on your offer to help clean it up. But if you don't have any evidence for me by this time tomorrow, the Radical Wave is suspended at Westport High. Do I make myself clear?"

"Crystal clear," I said solemnly, thinking that twenty-four hours was an awfully short stay of execution.

When the meeting was over and we were walking out of the administration building, Alex and I told Mr. Horton that he'd put on a blockbuster performance.

"Do you really think so?" he asked.

"I think Ms. Elder was particularly impressed with the way you handled things," Alex added.

Mr. Horton smiled broadly, but then he stopped suddenly, lowered his sunglasses to peer directly at us, and said, "Ms. Elder and I have a purely professional relationship, of course."

"Of course," Alex and I agreed, nodding vigorously.

"So we've got twenty-four measly hours," Alex said, turning back to me. "Assuming Geier did it, how do you suggest we nail him?"

"This is my exit, boys," Mr. Horton said,

tipping his hat to us as he turned to head for the drama building. There were only about five minutes left in first period, so it was obvious that he was bailing out on us. But we could hardly expect him to solve all our problems.

Alex and I sat down underneath the huge alumni oak tree, which was located in a hollow on the green between the administration building and the auditorium. "Why is this happening to me?" I asked as I buried my head in my hands.

"It's not just happening to *you*," Alex said. "The Wave belongs to a lot of people. . . . And I hate to beat a dead horse, bud, but I don't think any of this garbage would've happened at all if you'd taken my advice and stuck to your own crowd all along, you know?"

I knew. *Boy*, did I ever.

"Rumor has it," I said after a long, thoughtful silence, "that Big Wave Dave is planning a comeback in the spring elections. He'll need our full support, which means of course that I'll have to set my own political ambitions aside."

Alex looked totally surprised at first, and then he started to laugh. "A most excellent gesture on your part. It's about time the big guy returned!" he exclaimed as we exchanged a high-five.

A most excellent gesture, maybe—but would it be enough to get Vivian back?

Fourteen

Virtually every member of the Wave spent the rest of the day conducting interviews and listening in on conversations, trying to gather any information that might help us nail the weekend vandals. During a meeting in the park after school, we found we'd gotten absolutely nowhere.

"This is bogus! I want to waste the dudes who trashed our club!" Sandbar Sam declared angrily. Several students echoed his sentiments, which made me nervous because Dean Phelps and Officer Dembro were standing right across the street, watching us closely.

"Just chill, Sam," I said gently. "They *want* us to freak out. They want an excuse to break the Wave. But we can't play into their hands, you know? Don't fight it—ride it. If we can't bag the culprits by tomorrow, then maybe we'll have to shut down for a while, but we'll be back!"

"Damn straight," Spider said. "And the last thing the suits expect us to do is to handle this thing with class, you know?"

Eric Schaefer stood up, eyed the crowd

nervously, and said, "I've been thinking, though. How do we know for sure that one of us didn't do it?"

"Are you spun or what?" Dizzy Danny responded indignantly. "Sabotaging your own club would be like coating your board with superglue. You'd wipe out along with everyone else!"

"Look," I said. "Phelps is waiting across the street for volunteers. Now's our chance to show him what the Wave is really made of. How many of you'll come and help Alex and me clean that crud off the school walls?"

No hands went up at first, and my heart sank like a stone. But then Sam got up and said, "Come on, people! This is our chance to make a full-rail bottom turn!"

That roused the surfers, and the rest of the crowd followed their lead. Our group of twenty-five true believers then marched en masse across the street to confront Dean Phelps, who seemed a little blown away by our show of solidarity. He and Officer Dembro led us to a room full of cleaning supplies, brushes, and paint, and began to pass them out. We divided the materials among various work crews and fanned out around the campus.

We worked like maniacs, scrubbing and painting, painting and scrubbing. Alex had to cut out early to go to work, but he returned on his bike about ten minutes later to tell me that my bike tires had been flattened. "You want me to go get you a pump?" he offered.

I shook my head. "Don't sweat it. I don't want to make you late for work. I'll take the athletics bus home and deal with it later."

"The jerks just won't let up on you, will they?" he said disgustedly.

"That's what makes 'em jerks," I said with equal disgust. As he rode off I returned to my work with a burst of angry energy. Flattening my tires! How low can you go?!

By five o'clock, when Dean Phelps began to call the work crews in, most of the graffiti had been wiped out or painted over.

"Looking good, huh?" I said to Dean Phelps just before I boarded the last athletics bus.

He nodded and surprised me by grinning a little. "I certainly didn't expect so many hardworking volunteers," he admitted. But then his grin flattened out and he added, "Of course, even if we've eliminated the conse-quences, we still have to deal with the cause."

"Yes sir, I know," I said grimly as I boarded a bus full of hostile athletes.

The athletes were mostly football players, and they all looked sweaty and sullen. As I began to walk down the center aisle, several players imitated the distinctive hiss of a spray-paint can. And then I saw Mike Geier leering at me. I had forgotten about *him* being an athlete! I had a sudden urge to turn and run, but there were a few other Rad Wavers on the bus and I knew I'd never live it down if I bolted.

I headed for an empty seat near the back of the bus and tried to ignore the sound effects, taunts, and hand gestures that followed me on my seemingly endless trip to solitude. Fullback Jed Van Leezwen tried to intimidate me by flexing the muscles on his forehead (How did he *do* that?), but I pretended not to notice. I sank down onto the hard-packed green vinyl and looked out the window, hoping to find escape in the dusky late afternoon sky.

Nobody said anything to me for a while after the bus got moving, and I was actually beginning to think that I would make it home without any big hassles. As usual, I was being overly optimistic.

213

"So I see you and your low-life friends tried to clean up your little mess," Mike said as he sat down just across the aisle from me. He was a large, muscular sort of guy when you got right down to it.

I ignored him at first, so he repeated himself.

Don't fight it—ride it, I reminded myself. "Thank you for noticing, commissioner," I said quietly.

Mike looked around at his athlete friends for support. "He called me *commissioner*," he said, as if this were the gravest of insults.

"Durant seems to think he's the king of the school these days," one football player said contemptuously.

"More like *queen* of the school," Mike said. Several players laughed and exchanged five-step handshakes. I let the jab pass and began to weigh the pros and cons of leaping out the window of a moving school bus.

"Are you deaf?" Mike said and then repeated the insult. When I still didn't respond, he said, "Look at the yellow stains on his shirt. What'd you do, Durant, pee on yourself?" The laughter which followed this clever remark was loud and boisterous.

The Rad Wavers on the bus were watching

214

me expectantly. They began to look embarrassed and disappointed by my silence, and I started to weaken. "No, Mike, that's not a problem for me," I said. "But I heard you were *masticating* in the cafeteria again today. How'd it feel?" There was a moment of stunned silence, followed by laughter and cries of "queeb" and "pervert." Mike was *furious*.

"You're so ugly," he said, pulling out his heavy artillery, "that your mother had to sit you in a corner when you were a baby and feed you with a slingshot."

The crowd laughed and applauded.

"Oh yeah?" I said. "Well, your birth certificate was a written apology from a condom factory!"

The crowd laughed and cheered so loudly that the driver, Ms. Floreani, threatened to stop the bus.

When things had calmed down a bit, an enraged Mike turned back to me and said, "So I hear you couldn't even hold onto a hosebag like Vivian Chandler. What'd she do, up her rates on you?"

I freaked! I literally leapt across the aisle and started pounding on his head. I had the advantage of surprise for only about ten seconds, though, and then Mike knocked me out of his seat and pinned me to the floor. As he started to shower me with punches and a sickening fireworks show lighted up my head, I realized that I was actually very much in love with Vivian.

By the time the bus had stopped and Ms. Floreani (with the help of several students) had pulled Mike off of me, I was fantasizing about my final crawl to Vivian's doorstep, where I'd beg her forgiveness, declare my love, and then die at her feet.

"You're both suspended!" Ms. Floreani screamed in a voice that sounded like the cry of a cat caught in a storm drain. She was a stooped, wrinkled woman with a bowl-shaped shock of white hair and thick, black-rimmed glasses. (It was rumored that when she'd started driving the bus, many decades ago, she'd been a raving beauty with the voice of an angel.)

We both began to argue with her, but she cut us off. "Give me your names and home phone numbers, and I'll pass them along to the dean. And then I want you to sit down and shut up or I'll throw you off this bus right now!"

So we both sat down. Mike looked virtually untouched, while I, as many spectators eagerly pointed out, looked like death warmed over.

"But I don't understand it," my mother said as she dabbed at my facial cuts and scrapes with a cotton swab drenched with hydrogen peroxide. "Why would you get into a fight to defend the honor of a girl you'd broken up with?"

The peroxide stung. "She left *me*, Mom," I said, jerking my head away.

My mother stared at my image in the bathroom mirror. The damage to my face looked worse than it felt. "Girls confuse you, don't they, dear?" she said sympathetically.

"He *may* be confused, but he's *definitely* been suspended for three days," my father said as he appeared at the bathroom door.

"Three days!" I protested, horrified at the prospect.

"That's correct," my father said sternly. "I just got off the phone with your Dean Phelps, and he said that a three-day suspension is the standard punishment for all parties involved in a fight of this nature."

I was *toast*. There was no way I could save the Wave now. "I guess I blew it," I mumbled.

"I guess you did," my father said. "This

sort of thing wouldn't happen if you took your medication."

Mom and I turned to him and said at the same time, "It's *Gretchen* who takes the medication!"

At dinner, which featured an exquisite blend of macaroni and processed "lite" American cheese, the subject of my fist fight and suspension was studiously avoided—that is, until Gretchen excused herself to go to the bathroom and returned to the table with her face covered in Band-Aids.

Dana and Gretchen laughed themselves sick, and even Mom began to titter a little. Dad and I exchanged mature, disgusted looks, but then we busted out laughing, too.

"Mike Geier had it coming to him, in my opinion," Dana said when the laughter had died down.

"It sounded to me as if both boys were at fault, at least according to what the bus driver told your Dean Phelps," Dad said.

"Yes, Daddy, but Mike stepped over the line. He got *too* personal," Dana pointed out. I wasn't sure why she was taking up my defense this way, but I really appreciated it.

"I see," Dad said, sounding a little annoyed. "You're impressed with your brother's actions because he defended a girl's honor. Very chivalric. But this same kind of misguided chivalry, taken to its logical extreme, leads to drive-by shootings."

We all regarded him with stunned looks. "That's entirely too harsh, Derek," Mom said.

"Is it, Karen? I don't believe so. If you'd had a gun in your backpack on that bus, T.J., would you have been tempted to use it?" he asked.

The question came way out of left field, but the answer that immediately came to mind was frightening. "You've made your point, Dad, okay? I'm sorry. It was stupid to jump the guy, and the evidence is all over my face. But he got on my case and wouldn't get off, you know? Sort of like you're doing right now."

My father gave me a sharp look but said nothing.

"I start out this nightmare day with the discovery that some jerks have painted my club's name all over the school. I stay after school to clean up the graffiti, and then I'm forced to ride home on the athletics bus because some bozo has let the air out of my tires. So I'm sitting there on the bus totally exhausted, minding my own business, when this moron who needs three of his four brain cells just to sit upright starts ragging on me. I wasn't exactly Mr. Rational by that point, you know?"

My father mulled that over for a few minutes.

"Did you tell that to the bus driver?" my mom asked.

I shook my head. "Ms. Floreani wasn't interested. It's not her job to ask *why* it happened."

"Ms. Floreani was the driver? That woman would have trouble describing her own dashboard, much less an altercation. It sounds to me like there were a lot of mitigating circumstances, which should be taken into consideration, Daddy," Dana said in her best lawyerlike manner.

Dad nodded thoughtfully. "I'm going to call your dean back," he said to me, "and see if I can't get your punishment reduced accordingly. If all else fails, I'll call Rich Fremont. I'm sure I can reason with him, even if his doctorate is in education."

"Thanks, Dad," I said gratefully. I was way stoked—my dad was actually going to bat for me!

220

We were eating dessert when the doorbell rang. I went to answer it, and when I opened the door and saw Vivian, I just about keeled over. I announced to my family who it was, excused myself, and then quickly went out on the porch and shut the door behind me. "Hi," I said sheepishly.

"Hi, yourself," she said. She was wearing old blue jeans, a Mickey Mouse T-shirt, red heart-shaped earrings, and a nervous grin.

"What're you doing here?" I asked. "I mean, I can't believe you'd come to see *me* after the way I've treated you. If I were you I'd—"

She reached out and gently touched one of the Band-Aids on my face. "My phone's been ringing off the hook about what happened on the bus this afternoon. What you did was really sweet—and *really stupid*. He could've killed you."

I nodded. "I lost my head, though, 'cause I love you, Vivian. For *real*. And I'm sorry for being such a jerk. Janet and I are ancient history now, and I'm not a leadership council wannabe anymore. Can you ever forgive me for going wacko on you?"

She eyed me skeptically for a few moments, and then her expression softened and she said, "By God, I think you mean it!"

I nodded vigorously. She laughed, and then we hugged. It felt *so-o-o* good to hold her again. "I love you, too, sport," she said. "But listen up: Promise me that the next time somebody insults me, you'll keep your hands to yourself. I really don't go in for this caveman stuff."

"Me neither," I said. "Too painful."

We sat down on the porch steps and hugged and kissed and talked for a while, and when the conversation got around to the Wave, Vivian said, "But if you're right and Mike Geier *is* behind the graffiti, then he should be easy to snare."

"How do you mean?"

"Remember when we were kids and I used to win those dinghy races all the time?"

"Only too well."

"Well, I won by outthinking my opponents—by anticipating their next move and then using it against them. . . . So if *you* were Mike Geier, what would your next move be?"

I thought it over for a while and realized what she was getting at. "I'd probably spraypaint the school one more time, just to make sure that the Wave would die!"

"That's exactly what I thought, Watson," Vivian said with a smile.

Even if Mike *didn't* hit the school that night, we just might be able to trick him into a confession.

Fifteen I hid behind a thick hedge as Vivian went up to Mike Geier's front door and knocked. He lived in a large blue two-story house with a gabled roof. (It looked sort of like something left over from a '50s family sitcom.) The woman who opened the door looked as if she'd spent most of her life peeling onions. "Yes?" she said to Vivian.

"Hi, my name is Vivian Chandler. Can I speak to Mike?"

The woman smiled in that frosty, protective way that some mothers have and said, "I'm Mrs. Geier, Mike's mother. Mike was in a bit of trouble today, and he's not really supposed to entertain callers this evening. Is this important?"

Vivian looked into the hedge for an answer, and I gave her a thumbs-up. "Very," Vivian said to Mike's mother.

Mrs. Geier peered at the hedge, gave Vivian a puzzled look, and then disappeared for a moment. I poked my head out and said in an anxious whisper, "Don't look over here. You'll give me away."

"Do *you* want to do this?" Vivian asked in an annoyed tone, her arms akimbo.

"Do what?" Mike asked as he appeared at the door.

I ducked fast, and Vivian took a step back to hide her surprise. "Um, that is, do you want to talk to me?" she said, folding her arms and looking at Mike expectantly.

"Aren't you Vivian Chandler, T.J.'s squeeze?" Mike asked, looking bewildered.

"That's ancient history, sport," Vivian said nonchalantly. "I wouldn't hang out with that dweeb now if you gave me a winning lottery ticket. Actually," she said, assuming a coy expression and moving a step closer to Mike, "I came over here to thank you for putting him in his place."

I was biting my lip, trying not to laugh. A winning lottery ticket? This girl was *good*—but I hoped not *too* good, for her sake. I wanted Mike to keep his slimy paws to himself.

"Put him in his place? What do you mean?" Mike asked, stepping onto the porch and shutting the door behind him.

"I mean the way you pounded him on the bus and, of course, the graffiti. That was *brilliant*," she said with a sly smile.

Mike's jaw dropped a little. "How did you—" he started to say.

"How many guys at Westport High are sly enough to come up with an idea like that?" she purred.

"And you're *glad* we—?"

"I am." Vivian ran a finger across his chest. He had on a T-shirt emblazoned with GO TO HELL, WORLD—I'M A SENIOR!

"It took a lot of guts to do what you did," Vivian continued, "but somebody had to. T.J. Durant was out of control."

Mike watched Vivian's finger travel across his chest, and then he looked up at her and smiled in a self-satisfied way. "Yeah, I guess it did take a lot of guts," he agreed.

"I love a man who's not afraid to take a few risks," Vivian said, giving him a dreamy sort of look. I started to laugh out loud and had to bite my hand to stop myself.

Mike and Vivian turned to look at the hedge. Mike seemed alarmed, and Vivian was obviously very annoyed. "What was that?" he asked.

Vivian picked up a rock from beside the porch and threw it into the hedge. She nailed me in the chest, and to disguise my reaction to the pain, I did my howling cat routine. "It was just some stupid cat," Vivian said, shrugging. "Now where were we?"

Mike continued to look suspiciously at the hedge for a moment but turned back to check out Vivian. (This was all for a good cause, I reminded myself as I tried to control my jealous temper.) "You were telling me about what you love in a man," he said, putting his arms around her.

I couldn't believe this guy! I'd seen dogs who were more subtle. I was ready to come to Vivian's aid if things went too far, even if it meant blowing the whole scheme.

"Michael Douglas Geier!" his mother called from inside the house. "You are *not* to socialize this evening. And you need to finish your SAT math review!"

"Good move, Mom!" I whispered.

"Give me a break, Mom!" the lech pleaded.

Vivian extracted herself from his embrace and said, "I wouldn't want to interfere with something as important as your SAT math review, Michael."

"Call me Mike," he said, lowering his voice. "Look, we're going to do the school again tonight—just to put a few more nails in the coffin, if you know what I mean. The beauty of it is, Durant is sure to be the prime suspect since he's been suspended already. Get it?" he asked, sneering with pride.

I patted my tape recorder. We had him cold.

Vivian squealed with delight. "No wonder you're commissioner of education," she said. "You're a *genius*!"

"What can I say?" he asked. "Me and a few of my buddies are meeting at the tower just after 2:00 A.M. We have to go later this time because the police are keeping a closer watch on the school. Can we count on you to show up?"

"Michael?" his mother said, sounding more insistent this time.

"Coming!" he said, rolling his eyes at Vivian.

Vivian gave him a sympathetic I've-got-one-just-like-her-at-home look. "I'll be there, big guy," she said, reaching out and squeezing his hand.

Mike returned the gesture by slapping her on the butt, and it was clear by the look on her face that Vivian almost lost it. She recovered, though, with a half-hearted giggle. "*That's* private property, sport," she told him in a voice that was straining to stay casual.

"Right," he said, laughing at the concept of a female body as private property.

He was having only moderate success at keeping his tongue in his mouth. Things might have degenerated further, but an angry Mrs. Geier finally opened the front door.

"She was just leaving," Mike said in a panicked voice as he gestured at Vivian.

Vivian waved good-bye, and Mrs. Geier ushered her son into the house. Just before she closed the door, she turned and looked directly at me. I froze in terror. I'd been discovered!

She walked slowly over to the hedge. My heart raced like a rocket. My life was over. I was going to jail for sure! I had an urge to toss my tape recorder into the neighboring yard, but I reconsidered and stuffed it into the inside pocket of my jacket. I'd rather face Mrs. Geier's wrath than lose my precious evidence. Besides, what was she going to do, frisk me for hiding in her hedge? Get real.

She leaned down toward the hedge I was crouching behind and studied it closely. She looked directly into my eyes.

"Wretched boy!" she said disgustedly. I thought that was a little harsh. After all, she'd never even met me.

I was preparing to stand, my mind racing

to think up a convincing story (I was taping the sounds made by sleeping plants for my botany class. My pet python was loose again.), when she abruptly turned and walked into her house, slamming the front door behind her. "Michael," I heard her say as I waited for my heart to stop pounding, "you promised me that you'd trim those hedges *yesterday*!"

When I caught up to Vivian she was really steamed. "That scuzz put his hand on my . . . on me," she said, her eyes ablaze with anger. "That slug, that maggot, that oozing—"

"I get the idea, Vivian," I said sympathetically. "But you were great! Not only did you get him to confess, you even got him to set a perfect trap for himself."

Vivian took a moment to shift gears. "Do you really think I was good?" she asked, smiling a little.

"Academy Award material." I replayed the tape to prove it. The recording quality was crystal clear, but we had to replay certain parts over and over because we were laughing so hard.

"That . . . was . . . awesome!" Vivian said when we'd finally run through the whole thing.

"The best," I agreed.

"T.J., I have so much fun when I'm with you," she said as she wiped the tears of laughter from her eyes.

"Hey, the feeling's extremely mutual," I said.

We stood in the night shade of a California sycamore tree for a few minutes, talking happily and savoring our success.

"But how're we gonna trap him?" Vivian asked when we were done congratulating each other.

"Oh, *we* don't have to trap him. We'll let other people do it for us."

"Huh?"

I explained my plan to her, and by the time I finished, she was laughing again. "You have a twisted mind," she said. "I'm just glad you're using it for a good cause."

"Me, too," I said, and we shared a good-night kiss. She was warm and soft and smelled like a hedge. Actually, for the next few hours, the whole world smelled like a hedge.

When I got home, my dad told me that he'd talked Dr. Fremont down to a two-day suspension. "Your club, however, will still be disbanded as of tomorrow. I'm sorry, T.J.," he said, sounding like he meant it. I wanted to reassure him about the club, but if I told him about Mike Geier, the next thing I knew we'd be talking to the district attorney.

"No problem," I said, smiling. "Dr. Fremont was more than fair to us. Can I be excused now? I have to call some friends to arrange to get the homework I'll be missing."

My father gave me a puzzled look and threw up his hands. "I don't understand teenagers," he told my mother as I walked to my bedroom.

"Well of course you don't, dear," my mother said.

I spent the next hour and a half calling Alex, Sandbar Sam, Spider Martinez, Eric Schaefer, and several other key club members. They all seemed excited by the plan Vivian and I had cooked up, so I asked each of them to call other friends that they were *sure* could be trusted. I made it clear that everyone had to lay low until *after* the taggers made their move. I figured we needed a graffiti sample to prove our case.

I used a school district phone directory that I'd borrowed from the main office to find phone numbers for a few crucial teachers and administrators. (I used some bunched-up athletic socks and crinkled cellophane to disguise my voice. I made it clear that if they showed up too soon or surrounded the school with cops and security guards, they'd never catch the vandals in the act.)

By the time I was finished making calls, it was after eleven. I was so pumped up that I was practically bouncing off the walls. I knew I should try to get some sleep, but I just couldn't—partly because I was so hyped to have Vivian back and partly because I couldn't stand the thought of missing out on the spectacle I'd gone to so much trouble to arrange.

Then again, as Vivian had reminded me, I *had* been suspended. Under the circumstances, it would be stupid to risk being seen on campus at two in the morning.

I laid my head on my pillow and tried to relax, but dark thoughts began to trouble me. What if Mike Geier was on to Vivian? What if he'd figured out right away that it was me behind the hedge, and *he* was trying to set a trap for *us*? All those people I'd called might show up for nothing. Worse yet, Mike could paint the walls beforehand and then claim that he'd caught *me* in the act but I'd gotten away!

Still, we had the tape. What could he do about that? He could claim that he'd known he was being tape-recorded and had faked his conversation with Vivian in order to trick us! Or maybe he'd had his own microcassette recorder, and even now he was editing Vivian's comments to make it sound like *she'd* confessed to the vandalism!

I sat bolt upright in bed, grabbed a wad of Kleenex from a box on my nightstand, and wiped the beads of sweat off my face. I'd obviously gone lunar 'toons. If Mike Geier was even *half* as smart and creative as I was imagining, he never would've vandalized the school in the first place! I had to get a grip.

I finally turned the radio on low and listened to old love songs and thought about Vivian. No matter how things turned out tonight, I'd still have her. I loved her, and she loved me back. The thought was so comforting that it lulled me to sleep.

I woke up to the sound of tapping on my window. I arose with a start and tried to shake the clouds of sleep out of my head. *"T.J.,"* a voice said urgently. I turned and saw Vivian. From where I was lying, the glow from the streetlight behind her made her look like a beautiful ghost. She smiled at me and I smiled back. I wanted to reach out and pull her close to me. What a great dream!

But it wasn't a dream. It was 1:13 A.M., according to my clock-radio. I unlocked the window and slid it open. "Hi, T.J.," Vivian whispered. "I just couldn't stand it. I *have* to see them catch Geier."

It took about two seconds for me to see things her way. Since I'd fallen asleep with my clothes on, I was pretty much ready to roll. I just slapped some water on my face, combed my hair, swished some mouthwash, slipped on a jacket, pocketed a flashlight, and climbed out the window.

"Thanks, T.J.," Vivian said, giving me a kiss. "You're faster than a fireman."

"No big deal. Women come to my window like this all the time."

"In your dreams, maybe," Vivian said, and we both laughed.

We walked as quickly as we could to the high school, ducking behind parked cars and bushes whenever the occasional car drove by. We got the impression that other people were out and about, but if they were, they were keeping a very low profile. When we got to the high school, we saw a few cars parked in the student and faculty lots, but we didn't see anyone in them or around them. We went and hid behind the ESL trailers, where we'd have a good view of the tower area. In the dead of night, Westport High looked as if it might be haunted, and the faint footsteps and whispers we heard all around us definitely added to that impression.

I shared the thought with Vivian, and she shivered and said the sounds probably were from some of the people I'd called and that we should talk about something else. So then I shared my fear that Mike Geier might not show up and that maybe he was setting a trap for us. She surprised me by saying that the same thought had occurred to her. "But hey, T.J.—no guts, no glory," she reminded me with a brave, crooked grin.

"Yeah, it's worth a lot of risk just for the chance to catch those scumbags in the act," I said angrily, pulling out my flashlight.

"In the act of what?" a voice asked from the darkness behind us. I spun around and shone my flashlight into the face of David Whitworth. He raised an arm to cover his eyes. David Whitworth? I hadn't called David Whitworth! Heart attack central! So this *was* a trap, after all! I had to think *fast*!

"What're you doing here?" I asked suspiciously, determined to put the heat on him. "Have you come to cheer on your buddy?"

"Don't get smart, Durant," Dean Phelps said as he appeared at Whitworth's side. The dean was wearing a green jogging suit with white racing stripes and looked sort of like a turtle that'd lost its shell. "We got a tip that someone was going to vandalize the school tonight, and yours was the first name that came to mind. It looks like we were right on target."

Oh my God—*Dean Phelps*! So my worst nightmare *had* come true! I wondered, with rising hysteria about life's unfairness, if Vivian would be allowed to come visit me in prison.

I was ready to hold out my wrists and let Phelps slap on the cuffs, when Vivian said, "You've got the wrong guy, Dean-o. Look!" We all looked to the roof of the auditorium where Vivian was pointing and gasped at the vision of shadowy figures approaching the tower. We watched in disbelief as one of the figures raised an arm to the tower wall, a movement followed by the distinctive hiss of a spray-paint can.

"Well I'll be damned!" Dean Phelps said angrily. "Who's up there?!"

"Why don't you ask President Whitworth?" I suggested.

But David suddenly looked as innocent as a newborn puppy. "I don't know what T.J.'s talking about," he assured Dean Phelps.

"We'll find out soon enough who's responsible," Dean Phelps said ominously, using his walkie-talkie to order a small army of security guards over to the tower. He also instructed them to light up the campus as quickly as possible. Dean Phelps then headed to the tower himself, and we followed closely behind. As we got near enough to make out the faces of the vandals, David yelled, "Mike?!" in a shocked voice. Mike Geier was one of six guys up on the roof, and when he and the others heard Whitworth's shout, they started to run.

They were stopped, though, by an explosion of light. Students and adults began to pour out of their hiding places all around the central green, shining their flashlights on the tower. It was a dazzling display, and Vivian and I wordlessly hugged each other with joy and relief. One of the vandals, only temporarily intimidated by the lights, started to run, but the accusing beams followed him everywhere, and he finally gave up, hopelessly raising his hands into the air.

Suddenly, classroom and hallway lights came on all over campus. *"Busted!"* several students shouted gleefully, and the crowd, which I could see now was composed mostly of Rad Wavers, began to cheer.

"What the—" Dean Phelps began to say. But then he lapsed into silence, apparently overwhelmed by the sight of so many students breaking curfew.

"Stay right where you are!" a familiar voice boomed at the culprits through a megaphone. It was Mr. Horton! And Ms. Elder was at his side, holding a halogen light the size of a bazooka. (I'd wondered why Ms. Elder wasn't at home when I called.)

The sorry six stood against the upper wall of the auditorium, looking like gangsters in a police lineup: Mike Geier and five other brain-dead degenerates.

"Looks like some people owe our club an apology," Alex said as he came toward us from across the green with Robin at his side. Dean Phelps arched an eyebrow at me but said nothing. Robin and Vivian exchanged congratulatory hugs, and Alex and I shared a high-five.

Officer Dembro disappeared into the auditorium. He reappeared a few minutes later on the roof. There were more cheers and he led the six thoroughly shaken saboteurs away and two campus security guards picked up the abandoned spray cans. The creeps had been in the process of repainting our club name on the tower. The writing style was an almost perfect match with the graffiti we'd cleaned off the previous afternoon.

Dean Phelps turned to me and said, "T.J., I don't suppose you'd happen to know who was responsible for getting this crowd here at 2:00 A.M. on a school night?"

"Uh, well, the truth is," I said, turning to face David Whitworth, "I was actually just out doing some star-gazing. Of course, I *never* thought I'd see a black hole tonight."

"But I had nothing to do . . . nothing to do with what Mike—" David stammered, looking at me pleadingly. "Do you honestly think . . . honestly think that I'd—" He looked at Dean Phelps, faltered again, and then began to panic. "But I didn't know! I'd never have allowed this to happen!" he protested.

"No, Mr. President," Vivian said in a cool whisper. "Of course you wouldn't have."

Sixteen

"To Robin and Vivian," I said, crashing my cola can into Alex's cola can.

"To the two most *major* of major babes," Alex agreed as he returned the gesture.

It was Friday night, and both girls had family commitments, so Alex and I were batchin' it at his trailer.

Alex stuck a handful of cheese balls into his mouth and began to munch. "I hear they're sending Geier to Marina High," he mumbled.

"A true story," I said, tossing mini Chips Ahoy cookies into the air one by one and then catching them in my mouth.

Two weeks had passed since Mike had been busted. Old Mikey was getting a one-way ticket to social Siberia, and the other guys involved had been put on graffiti-cleanup duty for the remainder of the school year. David Whitworth, with Janet standing loyally at his side, had apologized to the student body at an antigraffiti rally called by Dr. Fremont. "While I didn't know about the vandalism, I may have unintentionally created an environment which encouraged such activity," David had said in an unusually quiet, humble voice. "To the extent that I am guilty, I apologize, and to the extent that I've disappointed you, I pledge to restore your trust in me in particular and in student government in general."

"Whitworth snaked his way right out of trouble, as usual," I said disgustedly after I missed one of my airborne cookies.

Alex belched sympathetically, crushed his cola can, tossed it into the recycling bin, and said, "He's one devious dude, no lie—a victim of the dreaded big-man-on-campus disease. And to think this same plague almost brought down my best friend!"

"*What?* Give me a total break here! There's no way I ever would've ended up like David Whitworth, not in a million years. I can't even believe you'd—"

"Why so cranky?" Alex asked as he abruptly stood up and walked toward the refrigerator. "Have we been skipping our *snacks* again?"

His question surprised me at first, but then I was overcome by guilt. "Is it that obvious?" I asked solemnly.

He nodded and shook his finger at me as

he opened the freezer door. "Don't you remember what you learned in health class, Thomas? A teenage male can survive for up to two weeks without normal food, three days without water, one day without seeing a babe, but only *six hours* without junk food. Don't tempt fate, bud."

He tossed me a virgin pint of Ben & Jerry's Chunky Monkey and a spoon. He soon returned to the couch with a pint of chocolate ice cream for himself, and we began to pork.

I waited until his mouth was good and full, and then I said, "Did I mention before that I've been asked by the council to serve as the new commissioner of education?"

Alex almost blew chunks, just like I'd hoped, and I rolled with laughter.

"Please tell me you're kidding," he said as he wiped a stream of ice cream from his chin.

I shook my head. "Scout's honor. It was David Whitworth's idea. He sprung it on me at lunch today. I suppose he meant it as a sort of peace offering. Pretty ironic, huh?"

" 'Ironic'? That's a nice clean word for it. . . . So what'd you say?" Alex looked annoyed and sort of worried.

I let him brood for a bit and then said, "Well, I gave it a lot of thought—for about ten seconds. But when push came to shove, I just had to turn him down."

"Good answer!"

"Yeah, well, I'm a pretty busy guy these days. With the Wave and drama and my school TV-news career, I already have too many distractions cutting into my time with Vivian, you know? Besides, Big Wave Dave is counting on my support this spring, and some council members just might see that as a conflict of interest."

"Some people are so narrow-minded about politics," Alex said with an ear-to-ear grin.

We ate some more ice cream. "You know, when you think about it, we're both pretty lucky that Janet dumped me," I said. "I mean, look at the awesome semester we've had! We've ridden the Wave to help some Radical causes, made a lot of new friends, gotten a little famous, outfoxed some vandals, and now we've *both* got steady girlfriends. How do you predict this kind of stuff?"

"You can't," Alex said matter-of-factly, waving his spoon at me. "If you wanna stay sane, young man, you've got to remember one thing: Anything can happen in high school—"

"And it usually does!" I chimed in, and then we both busted out laughing.